Old Dogs, Children, and Watermelon Wine

a novella

BY *James Michael Spiers*

 FriesenPress

One Printers Way
Altona, MB R0G 0B0
Canada

www.friesenpress.com

Copyright © 2022 by James Michael Spiers
First Edition — 2022

All rights reserved.

No part of this publication may be reproduced in any form, or by any means, electronic or mechanical, including photocopying, recording, or any information browsing, storage, or retrieval system, without permission in writing from FriesenPress.

ISBN
978-1-03-915429-2(Hardcover)
978-1-03-915428-5 (Paperback)
978-1-03-915430-8 (eBook)

1. FICTION, CHRISTIAN, FANTASY

Distributed to the trade by The Ingram Book Company

Dedicated To:

PAM
Much more than I deserve.

JODIE
Most generous person I know.

MATTHEW and SHERRI
They gave us three of the brightest stars in the universe:

TRISTA VANCE and RAINA

Table of Contents

PROLOGUE
AD 33 - 1

CHAPTER 1
THE CROSSING - 6

CHAPTER 2
BREAD AND WATER - 12

CHAPTER 3
THE HIGHWAY - 20

CHAPTER 4
SHELLFISH AND AVOCADO - 28

CHAPTER 5
ON THE FARM - 38

CHAPTER 6
THE MANSION - 45

CHAPTER 7
DINNER TIME - 52

CHAPTER 8
BACK TO SCHOOL - 60

CHAPTER 9
CITY LIFE - 68

CHAPTER 10
ONE OVER PAR - 79

CHAPTER 11
THE DARK - 88

CHAPTER 12
LOST IN THE SIXTIES - 98

CHAPTER 13
ROCK MY SOUL - 109

CHAPTER 14
DESERT STORM - 119

CHAPTER 15
BURNT OUT - 124

CHAPTER 16
STRANGER EN ROUTE - 133

EPILOGUE
TODAY - 139

AUTHOR'S NOTE - 141

ACKNOWLEDGEMENTS - 143

CREDITS - 145

ABOUT THE AUTHOR - 147

A STORY OF HEAVEN

My frail attempt to deter its reader from
the alternative.

PROLOGUE

AD 33

His appearance was no different from any other, his upbringing not unlike those he grew up with. He was not seen as handsome or otherwise. He stood little more than average height, and walking down the street, he would not be given a second glance. He was seen by others as one of them.

But he was not from their world.

His circle of friends was small, and he often associated himself with those seen by many as undesirable.

People stayed away from those who were sick for fear of becoming so themselves, but this man had no such fear. He would seek out those who were sick and, after spending time with him, they would become well.

Many were mystified by all he was able to do and were afraid. Those he was close to marveled at his powers and constantly sought his presence. One evening they gathered around him and pressed him for answers.

"You say you're the son of that carpenter," one of them asked, "but who are you really?"

"My brother has been sick for many years," another said. "Now he is well. He said it was you, he said you made him well."

They spoke of other miraculous things he had done. When they had become quiet, he asked them to sit on the ground. When they were seated, he sat with them and began to speak.

"I've been sent by God and have the power to do many things, but my main purpose is not to heal the sick. There's a debt that needs to be paid and I have to pay it."

He paused a few moments. "I'm the only one who can pay it."

"How much is the debt?" One of them asked.

Once again, he allowed a little time to pass. "They're going to kill me."

His friends gasped as one. "Who's going to kill you?" one of them shouted. "Tell us who it is; we'll stop them."

"No," he replied. "You cannot stop them."

Those who were afraid of him, his enemies, received word that he was professing to be God and arrested him.

| Old Dogs, Children, and Watermelon Wine |

They tried him without representation and found him guilty. Then they took him to the outskirts of town and killed him.

His friends, powerless to do anything, went away to a quiet place and mourned together.

After a few days they went to find where their friend had been buried. They asked where his body might be found and were told that, a little way outside of town, his body had been placed in a small cave and a giant rock had been rolled across the entrance.

The small group made their way out of town and, after a little searching, came across the burial place. As they approached the cave, they saw that the entrance was unprotected; the rock had been pushed to one side. They ventured closer, and one of them looked inside. After a few moments, he turned and looked back at anxious faces.

"Its empty," he said. "There's no one there." They looked at one another, but no one spoke. Then they turned around and walked away.

Upon reaching an overhanging tree, one of the group stopped and sat in the shade. One by one, the others joined him. They waited silently, staring at the ground. First their friend was killed, then his body stolen. Without him they were at a loss as to what they should do.

Then they heard his voice.

"I'm over here."

They looked up, and directly in front of them was the one they believed they had lost. As they stared at him, not yet believing what they were seeing, he sat with them as he had done many times before. They listened intently as he spoke to them.

"The debt has been paid, and the God who sent me has brought me back. But now I must leave you and return to my world. When I get there, I'll prepare a place for you. When your time comes, you will leave this world and join me in mine. Tell others about me. Tell them if they believe, as you do, that I was sent from God, when they leave this world, there will be a place for them also."

He raised himself to his feet, looked at each one of them and smiled. Then, without another word, he walked away.

They watched him go. No longer the subject of a criminal trial, no more did he walk with his head bowed, humbled by a guilty verdict. He had been abused and broken but had remained silent. Not anymore.

He walked away from them, his stride confident, his posture upright. No more did people overlook him. As he passed by them, his presence and his demeanor demanded their attention. He strode away, his footsteps creating a wisp of dust from the dry earth.

Then he was gone.

One from the group stood, his eyes searching after the one who had left them. In little more than a whisper, the others heard him say.

"Master."

Another got to his feet, and he too looked out across the dry land.

"He wasn't sent from God," he said.

"He is God."

CHAPTER 1
THE CROSSING

I placed the book on the table in front of me and stretched my arms above my head. From my window seat I turned and looked through the glass. Two dozen eyes were fixed upon me. I never ceased to be amazed by how they could detect such a movement given the distance that separated us. They continued to watch me for a while. Then, satisfied that I was not a threat, one by one, the elk lowered their heads and continued to graze.

I looked beyond the tall, gangling animals to the fir trees at the bottom of the field, which served as a front to the gently sloping hills. While I had never ventured farther than the tree line, I knew that a river flowed between the stand of trees and the hillside. A river I had not yet seen.

I got to my feet, once again alerting the elk, and made my way to the back door. I stepped outside, walked around the building and down the driveway to the gravel road. I crossed the road and opened the gate that allowed me into the field. The elk made their move. With ungainly elegance, they cantered to the far side of the field and watched me from there. The fir trees were ahead of me. I made my way toward them.

Halfway across the field, I began to feel the pain in my legs, a feeling with which I was becoming familiar. A few years before I had been in a motor vehicle accident; both my legs had been irreparably damaged. Since then, walking only a short distance caused pain.

When I was close to the tree line, I looked around for a place to sit. Spotting a tree stump sawn off flat, I walked over to it and sat. Immediately, relief began to set in. I knew that after a while the pain would subside and I'd be able to continue my walk.

It was a pleasant day in late spring, and walking across the field, it had felt quite warm. Sitting in the shade of the trees felt cooler, almost chilly. I leaned forward, rested my chin on my knuckles, and closed my eyes. The pain eased and was almost gone. A few more minutes of rest and I'd be able to move on.

The stand of trees was thick and tall, but with little undergrowth, so it was not difficult to walk through. I came out on the other side sooner than I expected and found myself at the top of a steeply sloping bank. At the bottom of the bank was the river, which I knew to be there but had never seen before.

Cautiously, I made my way down the bank, using a zigzag pattern as a way to reduce the slope as much as possible. I was relieved that the ground felt solid; it seemed unlikely that I would slip and fall. I reached the bottom and crossed a narrow strip of flat, bare earth and stood beside the river.

The water was dark. I was unable to determine how deep it was. Its leaden semblance did not allow me to see below the surface. The flow of the water was slow, methodical, lifeless. An occasional ripple seemed to offer a promise of some life, but it came to nothing. Only a faint swirl on the surface spoke of the current below.

The water had no appeal. It appeared cold and uninviting. Above, the sky was bright and blue, yet the dark water reflected none of its light and colour. Looking across the river gave welcome relief from the depressed water. The lush grass reached to the water's edge and extended back to the benched hillside with its gentle, easy slope reaching up to an ever-brightening sky. I looked at the hillside and the sky above. This was the view that I had from my window at home, but standing where I was now, the clarity of what I had looked at so often was multiplied ten times.

The pain had returned to my legs, but inexplicably I felt drawn forward. I took a step, then another. My feet touched the water, yet I continued to move ahead. The water reached my ankles, then my knees. I continued on. The water was soon up to my waist. I began to feel the current and suddenly became very cold. When the water reached my shoulders, I knew I should go back, but any attempt I made to turn around only took me deeper. The water touched my face, cold and unfamiliar, its surface almost at the level of my eyes.

Suddenly, there was a swelling of the water. It rose up, and in an instant, I was submerged and in complete darkness. I felt the current pulling me down stream and I was unable to fight against it. The cold, murky river had drawn me into its depths and was not about to release me.

Then all became still, as if the world had taken pause. The current and the pull of the water died, the cold left me, and I was no longer fearful. I had a feeling of nothingness, as if suspended in a void. I experienced a kind of peace that was unwelcome. A sense of suspense that lingered too long.

As I felt myself drifting away, there was a sudden flash of daylight, brilliant and warm. The water subsided and my head rose above the surface. I could see the river's bank a little way ahead of me, the easy slope of the hillside, and the expanse of blue above. I moved forward, slowly and tentatively, one step at a time. When the water was below my waist, I moved more easily. Moments later, I stepped up on to the bank and dry ground.

The earth and the air were warm, and the atmosphere embraced me. I looked around, one way then the other. The river, a ribbon of dark water, wound its way to the horizon, as did the grassy bank and the adjoining hills with the occasional fir standing tall on the slopes. The sky above remained cloudless, blue, and bright.

I turned and looked back to where I had come from, but I was unable to see the opposite bank. A mist had formed, blocking out everything on the other side. A thick fog, heavy and grey. It extended high above the trees, reaching up to the sky to the left and to the right, as far as the eye could see. The place from where I had come had disappeared. It was as if it had never existed.

I turned back and looked at the hill ahead of me. It looked like an easy walk, and I began to move forward. Then I stopped. Something didn't seem quite right. I looked down and checked myself over. The colour in my shirt and my trousers seemed to have faded. I couldn't believe that the river had washed the colour out. I hadn't been in there long, a few minutes at most. I reached down and felt my trousers, then my shirt. They were dry. That was odd. The air was warm, but surely my clothing could not dry that quickly. Having no explanation, I put the enigma out of my mind and returned my focus to what lay ahead. My goal was to reach the top of the hill.

| Old Dogs, Children, and Watermelon Wine |

As I walked I became increasingly captivated by the sky above. Progressively, it grew brighter the higher I got. It was an expanse that seemed to be its own source of light.

I had been walking for some time when I realized there was no pain in my legs. Normally, by now I would have been looking for a place to sit and rest until the pain subsided.

Now I felt like I could walk forever, run a marathon even.

What a feeling! No pain.

I continued on. As my steps took me higher, the sky, clear, blue, and wide claimed my full attention.

CHAPTER 2
BREAD AND WATER

"Can we offer you some refreshment?"

I turned abruptly and looked in the direction from which the voice had come. Seated at a picnic table in the shade of a leafy tree were five people, three men and two women. I was a little surprised; I wasn't expecting to see anyone else out here. I didn't know why; it was not as if it was my own private hillside, and it was a pleasant spot for a picnic. I walked a couple of dozen steps and stood beside the picnic table.

"Thank you," I said, "That would be nice."

The man closest to me stood up. "I'm Paul," he said,

then turned to the others at the table. "This is Rachel, Olive, Danny, and Philip."

I introduced myself. "I'm Michael."

Paul sat down and invited me to do the same.

Rachel began to unpack a small bag, first plates, then glasses. "Its not much," she said. "Just some bread and water."

Just bread and water, I thought. Not much of a picnic. Prison food came to mind.

Rachel continued to unpack, placing two large pitchers of water on the table followed by a paper bag containing the bread, which was distributed around the plates. Once the glasses were filled with water, we were ready for . . . lunch, if bread and water could be called lunch.

But we were not quite ready. Danny suddenly spoke out. "Oh, God who gives us all things, thank you for providing for us again to-day."

Grace had been said. Bread and water only, yet they felt it necessary to offer up thanks to God.

A plate of bread and a glass of water was placed in front of me, and we began lunch. I took a sip of water. It had a refreshing quality that I'd never experienced before. It was cool and tasted alive, without flavour, but if I could only drink one drink for the rest of my life, this would be it. The bread on my plate had the appearance, not of regular bread, but more of a flat bread. I took a bite. The texture was flaky, and the bread seemed to dissolve in my mouth. It had a flavour that was somewhat familiar. My mind made the effort to recall. Then it came to me. An East Indian gentleman had given me a piece of bread one time, bread he had made himself. "Try this," I remembered him saying. I recalled the wonderful taste of that bread. I had tasted nothing like it, before or since, until now.

As I was enjoying the refreshments, I asked them where they were from. "Do you live on the other side of the river like me? I'm pretty sure we've never met before."

Danny looked up at the hilltop. "We live over there," he said, "on the other side of the hill."

I also looked up. "That's where I was heading," I said. "Is it worth the walk?"

They looked at each other, a hint of a smile on their faces as if they shared a secret, something I didn't know.

Then Olive spoke. "Yes, I would say its definitely worth the walk."

"So what's it like over there?" I asked. "Is it much the same as here? Is there a town or village within walking distance?"

"Actually, on the other side of the hill it's nothing like here at all," Philip said. "And it's not far to the nearest town, but you'll find out when you get there."

I looked at my wristwatch but, oddly, it didn't seem to be working. I turned to my companions "You know, maybe I should do this another day when I can make an earlier start. That way I'll be able to spend more time looking around. When I get back to the river, I need to find a bridge and that may take a little time. I really don't want to wade through the water again. On the way here I almost got swept away by the current. So, I think I'll just head back and return another day".

The group was silent for a few moments, then Paul turned and looked directly at me. "You can't go back," he said.

They were all looking at me, and I felt a little bewildered. "I can't go back?" I repeated. "What do you mean I can't go back?"

Paul assumed the role of spokesman for his friends. He looked up at the top of the hill. "We told you that we live on the other side of that hill. But we didn't always live there. We used to live where you lived and, like you, we crossed the river."

He paused, keeping his eyes on me. They were all watching me. "Once you've crossed the river there's no going back."

I was beginning to feel a little uneasy, fearful even. My mind went back to when I crossed the river. I began to suspect that what I experienced there was not reality as I knew it. The darkness below the surface of the water. The pull of the current. The cold and the fear followed by an uneasy peace, and that feeling of suspense. Then the inexplicable receding of the water, and the sudden daylight, brilliant and warm. Why were my clothes lighter in colour, and how had they become dry so quickly? How was it the pain in my legs had gone?

"But I need to go back, back across the river," I insisted.

"I have family there. They'll be missing me."

"Yes," Paul replied, "they will miss you, but don't worry. They know where you are; they know you're okay."

"Will I ever see them again?"

"Oh yes." Once again Paul looked at the top of the hill. "When it's their time, they will join you over there."

"When they get there, how will I find them?"

"You'll find them."

I looked around the group and my surroundings.

Just five ordinary people having a picnic on a grassy slope beneath a cloudless sky. Nothing out of the ordinary, yet there was a feeling within me with which I was not familiar.

I turned back to Paul. "I feel as if I've left one world and entered another." I said.

"That's exactly what you have done," he replied. "On the other side of that hill is your new world."

"So is that where I'll spend the rest of my life?"

"You could say that, but more accurately, its where you'll spend eternity." Paul shifted in his seat as if making himself comfortable before telling a long story.

"I'm sure that many times you have looked out at night and marvelled at the universe lit up before you. I'm sure you've wondered why it's there and what it holds. When you make your way down the other side of the hill, you will no longer be admiring the universe from a distance as you have done before. You'll be entering into the very heart of the universe itself. It's the place we call the heavens,

| Old Dogs, Children, and Watermelon Wine |

a universe made up of worlds created with us in mind."

Again, my eyes came to rest on the top of the hill. "So I'm not quite there yet," I said. "When I get over the hill I'll be in my new world, right?"

"Right."

"Where am I now?" I asked. "You say I've left the old world, but haven't yet reached the new world. What world is this?"

"You could call it the entryway," Paul said, "the approach to heaven, the way by which people need to come to get there."

I looked around. No golden gates hanging on towering granite pillars embedded with pearls. No army of trumpeters to greet me. And that suited me just fine.

Nothing but a gently sloping hill served as the gateway to the universe.

I looked at the people sitting around the table. "What are you doing here?" I asked. "What made you leave your world to come and wait here?"

"We come here from time to time." Paul said. "If it's not us it will be someone else. We're here for those, like you, who have crossed the river. We point them in the right direction, make sure they reach their destination."

"So you and others wait here and meet people before they enter heaven?" I said. "I thought that was St. Peter's job."

They all laughed.

"It might well be his job," Paul said. "I've never seen

Peter down here, but that's not to say he doesn't show up here from time to time."

I looked again at the hilltop, and suddenly I was anxious to make a move, to reach the summit. I placed my hands on the table in front of me and eased myself to my feet. I stood for a moment, then sat back down.

There was something I needed to know before I left. "Paul, tell me, when I get there, heaven, will I get to meet . . . the Master?"

"Of course," Paul said. "Everyone gets to meet the Master."

"How will I find him?"

Paul's response was short, to the point, and left me in no doubt. "He will find you."

I finished what was left of my bread and water and had never felt so refreshed. It was then that I felt a little guilty for having likened my lunch to prison food.

I looked around at the group. "Will I get to see you again?"

"I'm pretty sure we'll meet again." Paul said. "Eternity is a long time."

Again, my eyes were drawn to the summit. "Well, I suppose I should make a move."

They all nodded, and I stood and walked a few paces. Then I turned and looked at them; they were watching me leave. "Thanks for lunch," I said. "I never knew bread and water could taste so good."

They gave me a wave, and I turned and focused my

attention to the top of the hill.
 I didn't look back.

CHAPTER 3
THE HIGHWAY

At the top of the hill, I stood in awe of all that was displayed before me. A sky above, below, and all around. A soft expanse of blue without horizon. A sky decorated with stars and planets, spheres standing out with clarity in the brilliant light of day, showing up as clearly as if seen in the darkness of a night sky.

There were globes that appeared to generate their own light, and others that reflected that light. Stars reflected upon each other as if light upon light. There were spheres that were translucent and blurred with colour, appearing as soap bubbles blown through a ring. I saw planets that were solid, that had substance and earthly colour, varying shades of brown and green with areas of blue denoting bodies of water. It was those worlds, those solid globes, that projected a sense of reality in what was otherwise a magical universe. It was those worlds that I felt could be inhabited, worlds that the Master had placed throughout the universe. Worlds that he had prepared for his people, places where they would spend eternity.

I gazed out into the universe. I could see far, farther than I've ever been able to see before. I looked past the worlds, the stars, the planets, many of them seeming large and close to me, others smaller and farther away. I felt as if I was seeing through one galaxy and into the next. I looked into the distance knowing that, beyond what I was able to see, the universe continued on. As I watched, I gained a new understanding of all that surrounded me. The galaxies that made up the universe I saw now as the heavens; heavens made up of worlds built by God for his people. One of them was built with me in mind.

I looked around in search of a pathway or some easy route off the hilltop and down into heaven itself. Close by, I saw a narrow path that led downward, cutting at an angle across the hillside. I stepped onto the trail and began to make my way down. The farther down I got, the more engulfed I became in this glorious universe. Then I found what I was looking for, a grey strip of what looked like pavement leading away from the bottom of the hill and out toward the stars.

I reached the bottom of the hill and stepped from the trail and onto the pavement, a road of two-lane width. I walked a few paces, then stopped and looked ahead at the road reaching far away into the distance.

This was not a road that had been rolled out like a ribbon and just hung there in space. It had substance. It had grassy shoulders, verges that gave way to meadows scattered with wild flowers reaching out to form a horizon with the sky.

Heaven's highway. Not a highway to heaven, but a highway through heaven itself.

I began walking again, looking one way, then the other, and back again. This universe was alive, electrifying, and real. There were spheres that appeared close, almost on top of me. I felt I could reach out and touch them. Yet, in reality I knew they were far away.

I came to a fork in the road. The highway I was on continued straight ahead and another road of the same width branched off from it. I stopped and looked down this new road. It ran straight for a while, then swept away in a wide curve and disappeared from sight. I stood for a while wondering where it might lead to. It was there for a reason; it was a road to somewhere.

I continued on, admiring the meadows as I walked. Wildflowers were plentiful, mostly yellow, highlighted with red and white. Before long, I came upon another road that branched off before disappearing into the distance. I looked out and focused on one of the spheres, a globe that was solid and had substance, a world that I sensed was inhabited with people just like me. As I walked on, I passed other roads, roads that would take me away from the main highway, roads that would take me to new worlds. I was tempted to leave the highway and go in search of one of those worlds and the people who lived there. But I stayed with the road I was on.

The highway I was walking seemed like a world of its own, the fields, the flowers and the occasional cluster of trees, but my feeling was that it was just a highway to somewhere, not a home. A highway that led to worlds that made up the universe, and it seemed there was a road to each one of them. One of those roads led to my world, and it was my choice. I could choose my world.

For the first time I turned and looked behind me to see where I'd come from. There was no sign of the hill that I had descended just a short time ago. The highway extended back, then disappeared from sight. In the distance, the fields flooded out from the highway and the stars and the planets and the worlds remained unmoved in the expanse of blue. It seemed I'd only been on the highway for a short time. But perhaps it had been longer than I realized.

As I stood there, I felt as if I had lost all understanding of time and distance. The hill that I had crossed must be back there somewhere, but I'd left it far behind. It was no longer within sight. I turned and moved on.

Heaven's highway, a grey ribbon appearing as hard asphalt, yet it was surprisingly easy on my feet. I noticed an occasional flash or glint from its surface. Light was reflecting off the aggregate, tiny pieces of glass-like rock that made up the road's surface.

Again I looked around at the universe resting above green fields without hedges, walls, or fences, no containment of any kind. I heard a sound and stopped walking. Running water. I left the highway and walked through the grass and the flowers toward the sound. It became louder, and it didn't take long for me to find the fast flowing water. The stream was wide, almost a river, the water shallow and moving swiftly. Below the surface, I saw rocks, many of them streaked with colour, clean and washed smooth from generations of rushing water.

Through the flowing water, I detected movement below the surface, a flash of silver. Then I saw it. A magnificent fish moving effortlessly through the water.

Then I spotted another close behind, followed by a dozen more. So heaven's waterways contained fish. I didn't know why this surprised me. Why wouldn't they?

As I looked at the water, full of life and light, my thoughts returned to my crossing of the river, the river of darkness. I marveled at how different it felt standing where I now was surveying such an idyllic scene. I walked a little way upstream and watched the fish, admired the colour of the rocks, and absorbed the sound of the water's movement.

As I took it all in, I realized I had seen many streams like this before, shallow brooks with coloured rocks, fish, and rushing water. But here the light of the universe gave the water a brightness and clarity that I had never before experienced.

I moved to the waters edge and bent down low. Cupping my hand, I scooped up water and raised it to my mouth. That was it. The same water that Rachel had poured for me on the hillside before I entered heaven. Water that refreshed and seemed to regenerate life itself.

I made my way back to the highway and headed for the distant horizon. Refreshed by the water, I felt that I could walk far before I needed to stop and rest. But how far was far? How far could I go? And however far that was, how long would it take me to get there? How far could I get before I needed to rest and to sleep? Was there night? If there was, how often did it come? Was it then that I would rest and sleep?

Since I'd started upon the highway, I had seen no one. It was a quiet road, I'd seen no passing traffic. Traffic. I'd been walking heaven's highway for a while and for the first time I gave thought to the possibility of vehicles traveling this road. It was wide enough for two vehicles to pass. There would be no reason for a nice wide road like this if there were no vehicles to use it.

But were there vehicles in heaven? Cars, trucks; perhaps even motorcycles.

While I was unaware of how long I'd been on the highway, I believed I had already traveled a great distance. Perhaps there was no need for motorized transportation in heaven. Maybe everyone could just walk to wherever they wanted to go. But the idea intrigued me. Cars on heavens highway. A person could get somewhere really fast. Maybe I could hitch a ride, branch off on one of the side roads, and be in another world in no time at all. And that would be reasonable as it seemed that in heaven, there is no time. Or at least not time that could be measured.

I began to hope that before long I would meet someone else, another traveler or travelers. People who were on their way from one world to another perhaps. People who could tell me where I was going and what to expect when I got there.

I looked ahead at the road stretched out in front of me and, in the distance, I saw something, a tiny dot on the horizon. There was something out there, and I quickened my pace, anxious to find out what it was. As I got closer, I saw the occasional flash of light, sunlight it would seem, reflecting off a polished surface. As I strode toward my target, it began to take shape. I could make out its colour, and its lines became apparent. The closer I got, the slower my steps became. Then I stopped. Parked on the roadside was something that was not unfamiliar to me, but seeing it there came as a startling surprise. I was looking at something that surely must be from another world.

I stepped alongside and laid my hand on the rear fender. Then I moved slowly toward the front. It had two doors; a convertible with the top down. The paintwork was two tones of blue, with cream leather interior. I put my hand on the front fender, classic lines highlighted by polished chrome. Whitewall tires that I would never dare to kick.

It was a '57 Chevy.

CHAPTER 4

SHELLFISH AND AVOCADO

"She's a beauty, isn't she."

I looked around and saw two people, a man and a woman, sitting on a blanket spread out on the grass a little distance away from the highway. I walked over and stood beside them.

"I hope you don't mind," I said, "I was admiring your car."

"Not at all," the man replied. "She's worth admiring, there's not many of them left."

| Old Dogs, Children, and Watermelon Wine |

I looked back at the classic car and said, "I had my own ideas of what heaven might be like, but I never dreamed that I would come across someone driving around in the likes of a '57 Chevy."

They both laughed and the man said, "Me neither, but I came across this one and, well, I just had to have it."

"Why don't you sit down," the woman said. "We're about to have a bite to eat. I hope you will join us."

I seated myself on the corner of the blanket and stretched out my hand to the man. "I'm Michael."

The man took my hand and shook it warmly. "I'm Lucas." He looked at the woman, "And this is Lydia."

Lucas and Lydia were both what I would call older people, I guessed a little beyond middle age. They were wearing light, comfortable clothes, well suited to the warm summery day we were enjoying. Lucas had dark hair with a touch of grey at the temples. Lydia also had dark hair, straight and of medium length, cut to a little below her shoulders. I was captivated by the soft pallor of their skin, lightly browned but not by the sun. Their colouring came by origin of birth. Filipino perhaps. Their complexion and colour was something others attempted to manufacture . . . without success.

This was an opportunity I'd been hoping for, to meet someone, someone who had been here perhaps for some time, or at least for longer than I had.

"So Lucas, tell me what you're doing," I asked. "You're out here sitting on the grass about to have a picnic, and you have a car, a '57 Chevy no less, sitting over there on the roadside. Are you just out for the day, or are the two of you on your way somewhere?"

"Yes, we're taking a little break," Lucas replied. "We're on our way to a world called Aster. It's beautiful there at this time. In all of the heavens there is no known world that produces more flowers. In the fields the flowers grow as densely as grass grows in a meadow. Everywhere you look it's an ocean of colour. The bushes and the shrubs all produce flowers, thousands of species and varieties. Colours more than can be numbered. The trees will be coming into blossom now, trees that can be seen as far as the eye will allow, blossoms of colours never before seen. There are mountains there covered with blooms bottom to top, and fields of colour that reach out to clear water streams and rivers. Meadows that have the scent of... well, let me put it this way... that have the scent of heaven."

He paused to take a breath, and Lydia took the opportunity to cut him off. "Lucas, sorry to stop you when you're in full flow, but would you get the hamper from the car? I think we should eat now."

Lucas stood and made his way toward the Chevy. In moments, he was back and placed a hamper basket on the blanket beside Lydia. She lifted the lid of the hamper and removed a sealed container, then three china plates. These were followed by shiny cutlery and glasses.

"I hope you have enough," I said. "I'm sure you weren't expecting anyone to join you."

| Old Dogs, Children, and Watermelon Wine |

"Don't you worry, we have more than enough," Lydia said as she removed the lid from the sealed container. Lucas called for quiet before offering up thanks to God. He thanked God for the food and for just about everything else, including me, their "new friend." Had it been hot food that we were about to eat, it may have been in need of reheating by the time he finished.

"Please, help yourself to a sandwich." Lydia said.

"Thank you." I placed a sandwich on my plate and the bread looked the way I would expect bread to look. White with a lightly browned crust. I picked it up and the bread felt soft and fresh, very different from the bread I'd had on the hillside with Paul and his friends. I took a bite and right away recognized flavours I loved: shellfish, avocado, and lemon.

"Lydia, when you made these sandwiches how were you to know that you were preparing some of my favourite things to eat?"

"Just lucky I guess. I'm glad you're enjoying it. Would you like some wine?"

Ah, wine! I didn't need to be asked a second time. "That would be wonderful."

Lydia took an insulated flask from the basket and set it down, then carefully placed three glasses on the blanket. She removed the top from the flask and poured the wine, half filling each glass. Its clarity was flawless, its colour a pale pink. I took a sip. It was chilled and dry, and the fruit lingered on my palate. I savoured the moment. Then

I had to ask. "What is this? What wine is this? I don't recognize the taste."

"I made it myself." Lucas said, a hint of pride in his voice. "It's watermelon. Watermelon wine."

I leaned back and gazed into the sky, a living universe of which I was a part. I felt as if I'd arrived. Here I was, sitting on a blanket on the ground with two of God's people, eating shellfish and avocado and drinking watermelon wine. Heaven indeed.

Lydia turned to me. "So what are your plans Michael? Are you heading anywhere in particular or just out for a walk?"

"I don't know where I'm going," I replied. "I haven't been here very long, just arrived actually, and in need of all the help I can get. But first, tell me about you. Where do you live? Do you have a permanent home?"

"Oh, yes," she said. "We live in Celosia. We have a small house there. Celosia is a world of mountains and wildlife with many lakes and rivers. Its a small world with few inhabitants, people who like a quieter life, a life without hustle and bustle."

"Are there many worlds in the universe that are inhabited?" I asked. "And how are they different from the world that you live in?"

Lucas took over. "Looking around, you see stars some of which give light and heat, and there are worlds out there, many of which are inhabited, but many are not. What I do know is there's a place for everyone." He paused to take a bite of his sandwich and a sip of wine. I did the same.

"The worlds are different, one from the other," he continued. "When you leave one and enter another, it really is like being in another world. There are those who are always traveling from one world to another, but to visit them all would surely take longer than eternity itself."

"Tell me about the worlds you've been to," I asked.

"Aster, where we're heading is our favourite place to visit, what with all the flowers, but each world has its own beauty, its own attraction. Bellis is a world of rich farmland and vibrant cities, and they produce food for many of the worlds around them. Many people there live in fine mansions."

"You said you lived in a small house," I said, "How is it that you live in a small house, and others get to live in mansions?"

Lydia laughed. "Don't be thinking that we feel hard done by. We live in a small house in a small world because we choose to. Mansions and city living is not our style. If it was there would be nothing to stop us from going to a world like Bellis and living in the city or in a big mansion."

There was something I'd wondered about. "Tell me how did you come to live where you now live? How did you acquire your house, your home, and others their houses or mansions? How did that come about?"

Lucas looked away and into the distance before answering my question. "When the Master said he would prepare a place for us, he spoke the truth."

And that was all the answer I was going to get.

Lucas turned back to me and resumed his narrative. "And then there's Statice. We've never been there, but apparently while there are a few areas of green and water, its a world that remains completely covered with snow. Its cold too. However, the people we've met that live there love it. They say they wouldn't live anywhere else. It seems that, wherever they are, they can ski and skate and a whole lot more. People go there for competitions and tournaments, hockey and curling and the like."

As I listened to all of this, my thoughts were of visiting those worlds and discovering them for myself. But I could only go to one world at a time, and travelling from one to another would surely take a great deal of time. But then again, maybe I had all the time I needed.

"This highway, it seems very quiet," I said. "You're the only people I've met so far. Am I likely to meet others along the way?"

"Oh, yes, you'll meet others," Lucas said. "It'll be quiet though. People mostly stay in their own world and use the highway only when making the trip from one world to another. There are always lots of people travelling, but remember, it's a big universe with many highways. When you leave this highway and enter a world, you'll encounter many people, in the cities and at concerts and festivals. Then of course there are the big praise gatherings, hundreds of thousands of people, all in one place making noise for the Master. Now that is something you have to see."

Praise gatherings in heaven I'd expected. But concerts and festivals I hadn't given much thought to until now.

"So, you're on the way to the world of Aster," I said. "How far is it?"

Lucas rubbed his chin as if deep in thought. "How far is it?" he repeats the question to himself. "Hmm. I'm not really sure. Lydia do you remember how far it is to Aster?"

"No I don't," Lydia replied. "Never really given it any thought."

However far it may be, the distance didn't seem to concern them, but I persisted. "Well, how long do you think it will take you to get there?"

Lucas rubbed his chin again. "If we don't stop too often, we'll get there in good time, but if we get distracted or leave the highway for any reason, it could take longer. We'll see."

So, just as I suspected, in heaven there was no understanding of time and distance, and it was a feeling I'd had since I arrived. It seemed that I had been here only a short time and had traveled only a short distance, yet it was time and distance that my mind was unable to comprehend.

Since I'd started walking, I'd passed by stars and planets, spheres that were ahead of me when I started out, but which were now behind me. There had been no darkness, no night time; it was still the first day. How long would this day last? Would it end at all? I figured I'd find out sooner or later.

I finished my sandwich and took my last sip of wine and felt like I'd had a feast. "Thank you Lydia," I said. "That was wonderful."

"Good. I hope that will keep you going until your next meal," she replied.

My next meal. I'm not sure where it would come from, but I felt confident that it would come from somewhere.

"Well, we should make a move," Lucas said as Lydia began to pack up the hamper. I could easily have stayed longer. There was much more I wanted to ask, but I needed to let them go.

"Michael, you're more than welcome to join us if you wish," Lucas offered. "Come with us to Aster."

"Thanks, Lucas. I'm tempted, but I think I'll keep walking. After listening to you talk about other worlds I'm thinking I'd like to go to Bellis, I'm keen to see the farmland there and visit the city, maybe see a mansion or two." Suddenly I had a thought. "Bellis is another world. How will I find my way there?"

"I have a map," Lucas said. "You can have it. When we get to Aster, we can pick up another one. You can get maps in any of the towns or cities."

"Great."

I bent down, picked up the hamper, and made my way toward the car as Lucas and Lydia folded the blanket. Lucas opened the trunk, and the basket and blanket were placed inside. He gave me the map and a hearty handshake. After a hug from Lydia, they were ready to leave.

"Well, Godspeed, as they say," Lucas said.

"You too," I replied.

They got into the car, and it began to move away. Slowly at first, then it gathered speed. Before long, the Chevy had disappeared into the heavens.

CHAPTER 5
ON THE FARM

I studied the map and found the road that would take me to Bellis. I needed to stay on the highway for some time before I branched off onto the road that would take me to another world. I put the map in my pocket and began walking.

As I walked, I continued to be enthralled by the universe that surrounded me. Sooner than expected I came upon what I was looking for: the road to Bellis. It forked off to the right and I left the highway and began heading in a new direction. The road was no different to the one I'd been on, the fields either side the same lush green,

| Old Dogs, Children, and Watermelon Wine |

littered with yellow, red, and white. Yet I was looking at everything from an unfamiliar position.

Everything seemed a little different. I was seeing the heavens from a new perspective, a universe that appeared to change depending upon where it was viewed from.

I looked at the road ahead. Something was coming toward me, another vehicle. As it approached, I wondered what it might be this time. A Cadillac, perhaps? Or maybe a Rolls Royce? As it got closer, I realized it was a make I didn't recognize.

The car came to a stop beside me, the windows rolled down, and I was confronted with half a dozen smiling faces.

"You okay?" the driver shouted. "You're not lost or anything?"

"I don't think so," I replied. "I'm going to Bellis. Am I on the right road?"

"Stay on this road and you'll get there," he said, then added, "Gotta get going. Don't want to be late for the game."

The car pulled away, arms waving from the windows, all of them clearly excited to be going to the game. Whatever that game may be. They were driving away from Bellis, so the game was obviously being played in another world.

Before long, I saw another vehicle coming toward me and another not far behind. As they passed by, we exchanged waves but neither vehicle stopped. Perhaps they were on their way to the game. Whatever that game may be.

The planets and stars around me changed little; they didn't seem to get any closer or become farther away. Except for one.

There was a world ahead of me that, as I walked, was getting closer and becoming larger. I was walking toward it, but it too seemed to be advancing upon me. I began to make out land mass and bodies of water, and I determined that what had become an enormous sphere suspended ahead of me was Bellis, the world of rich farmland, vibrant cities and fine mansions. The road I walked was leading me straight to it.

As I moved forward, the world ahead of me was slowly taking over the depth and breadth of my vision. Little by little, this world called Bellis was eclipsing all other stars, planets, and worlds that just a short time before had been within my sight.

I maintained my pace and kept my eyes fixed forward. Then, without drama, without fanfare, I stepped into a new world, a world with people living out eternity in the place of their choosing.

The road I found myself on was not unlike the one I had just left, but the fields on either side had changed. There were fields that were cultivated, the soil a rich red-brown in colour. In others crops were growing, wheat, oats, and oilseeds. As I moved on, I came to orchards on both sides of the road reaching out to the low hills in the distance. Many of the trees bore fruit; others had yet to produce.

| Old Dogs, Children, and Watermelon Wine |

Farther on, I came to vineyards, vines bearing grapes, red and white, some ripe for harvest, others yet to mature.

I came to a dirt track leading from the highway to a group of buildings some distance across the field. The buildings didn't look like houses; it looked more like a farm site. I wondered what might be inside those buildings. Farm machinery, I supposed. I already knew that people in heaven ate and drank, and I could see the crops around me, grain, oilseeds, fruit, and what looked like vegetables growing in the distance. So it was not unreasonable to suppose that they had farm machinery to cultivate the land and harvest the crops.

Although I had not seen any yet, perhaps there were also animals on the farm, livestock for meat. If people ate fish, I knew the streams and rivers were well stocked.

I looked at the vines as I passed by. The fruit was small; it would be some time before it reached maturity. As I admired the well-tended vineyard, I noticed a man walking between the rows. Every few steps, he stopped and reached into the vines with both hands. He appeared to be tending to the crop in some way.

I left the road, entered the vineyard, and made my way toward the man. As I approached, he lifted his head and, upon seeing me, smiled and said. "Hello there. Another beautiful day."

"Yes it is," I replied. "I hope you don't mind; I was just passing by and I wanted to find out what you're doing."

The man stopped working. "Just keeping up to date with the pruning. Must keep on top of the pruning, you know. Otherwise, the vines won't produce the way they should."

"Do you look after all these vines alone?" I asked. "What about the other crops back there, the fruit trees and the grain crops, are those your responsibility too?"

"They are, and the vegetable crops up ahead. In fact, everything on this road from here all the way to the city. But of course, I don't do it all myself. There are many of us that work on this farm; in fact, just about everyone who lives in this valley helps out in one way or another. At harvest time, lots of folks come out from the city and everything that needs to be done gets done. At the same time, they get all the food they need for themselves."

I surveyed the farmland around me. There was nothing difficult to figure out here. This man was a farmer, plain and simple.

I had more questions. "In addition to the crops, do you keep livestock, animals for meat?"

"No. There's no need for us to raise livestock, not here in Bellis. We have an abundance of wildlife; anyone is free to go out and hunt for food if they wish."

"What about machinery? What do you use to cultivate the soil and harvest the crops?"

He straightened his back and looked pleased that I had asked the question. "We have the best," he said. "Four-wheel drive, three-hundred horsepower. Everything we need to get the job done."

Old Dogs, Children, and Watermelon Wine

None of what I was seeing and hearing was new to me, it was all very familiar. Crops in the ground, tractors, cultivators, harvesters. People tending to the crops and gathering their food. But somehow it all seemed less demanding, a part of daily living to be enjoyed along with everything else, less complicated and unhurried. People caring for the land and the crops because it was the work they chose to do. People coming from the surrounding areas to gather fruit and vegetables for no other reason than to feed themselves and others.

Out on the road, a pick-up truck drove slowly by, and the driver sounded the horn.

The farmer gave the truck a wave. "That's John. He'll be on his way to check on the yellow plums. They'll be almost ripe by now."

The farmer turned to me and reached out his hand. "By the way, my name is Abel."

"Michael," I replied "Tell me Abel, Bellis is known for its rich farmland, vibrant cities and fine mansions. Do you live in a mansion?"

"I certainly do," he replied proudly. He pointed across the vineyard. "I live over there. My mansion is just out of sight, behind those trees. Walk with me while I finish pruning this row, then I'll take you to my home and show you around. You'll also get a chance to meet some of my friends and neighbours. We're having a little dinner party and you must join us."

We reached the end of the row and stepped out onto a grassy track. Turning away from the highway, we began the walk toward the trees at the foot of the hill. Abel looked at the vines as we walked, checking to see if anything needed his attention.

As the grass track gave way to a gravel driveway, we left the crops behind us.

CHAPTER 6
THE MANSION

The grass on both sides of the driveway was closely mown, manicured even, and the gravel was unlike anything I'd seen before. The small pieces of aggregate were multi coloured, as if each piece had been hand painted. Towering acacia trees on each side formed a shaded avenue, their delicate leaves fluttering in an undetectable breeze. My surroundings suggested that I was indeed approaching a fine mansion.

The coloured gravel took a turn, and as we rounded the bend a huge archway came into view. Two stone pillars reached upward, then, with an architectural curve, joined together in the centre. At the base of the pillars, low walls extended out from each one, decoratively built with glass lanterns at each end. It was a grand entrance, but no gates hung from the pillars. Anyone could walk freely in or out.

My pace slowed as I admired what was indeed a fine mansion. The archway served as framework for the building that lay beyond it, a house that was wide and high. Like the archway, it was built of stone and rock. The windows were large and there were many of them. While it appeared to be only two stories, its height could easily have accommodated four. A porch covered four wide steps that led up to the double entry doors. As we passed through the archway, I noted that each stone had been cut and shaped by a skilled craftsman and joined perfectly with those beside it.

We approached the mansion, and I admired first its roof of dark blue slate. Each piece cut to a different size, yet each fitted to those around it. The windows especially captured my attention, huge panes of crystal-clear glass edged with what looked like stained glass. Not individual pieces of different colour, but a continuous border of glass in which one colour blended into the next. Each window was framed by emerald- green rock, which highlighted the sand-coloured stone of the building. The entrance doors were of polished hardwood with shining hardware.

As the driveway approached the building, it became wider, allowing space for vehicles to park. Several cars were parked close to the mansion, a variety of makes and models sitting on the coloured gravel.

Abel pointed at the cars. "That will be a few of our friends here to help Monica prepare dinner."

"And who is Monica?" I asked.

"Monica and I have been here a long time, I arrived first, and she joined me a short time later. We've been here ever since."

I wondered for a moment just how long a long time was, but decided against asking the question.

We stepped up onto the front porch. Abel opened the door, and we went inside.

The entrance hallway was wide and extended to the full depth of the building. Its height was the full two stories. Daylight streamed down from four big skylights set in the roof. The floor was marble, veined with colour. The centre piece was a huge carved rock sitting in a wide circular basin. Water seeped from the rock and trickled musically into the basin below.

Several doorways led off from the entrance hall, and Abel steered me toward one of them. As we passed an open door, I saw about a dozen people working at what I assumed to be, preparing dinner.

"The kitchen," Abel said as we walked by. "We'll stay clear of there for the moment. Don't want to get roped into peeling potatoes or anything."

With more than a dozen people helping out, I wondered just how little this dinner party was actually going to be.

Across the hall from the kitchen, Abel walked through a large arched doorway. "This is the dining room," he said.

I followed him into the room and looked down its full length. It reached to the end of the building. At the far end was a wide carpeted staircase extending up to a balcony that wrapped around the room and provided access to rooms on the second level. As in the hallway, high up in the roof a row of skylights shed light on the dining room table, adding to the light that flooded in from the many windows around the room, windows of crystal-clear glass and edged with colour.

The dining table captured my attention. Its length was a little less than the length of the room itself, long and narrow with about twenty-five chairs on each side. Seating for fifty people. Each place was set with a silver mat, silver cutlery, and a scarlet napkin in a silver ring.

Crystal glasses of varying shapes and sizes lined the table from one end to the other, reflecting colour from the bowls of fresh cut flowers.

I turned to Abel. "A little dinner party, did you say?"

He laughed. "Follow me."

We walked the length of the table to the staircase. Unlike the entrance hall, the floor here was polished hardwood, dark and deeply grained.

We reached the stairs and made our way up. From the balcony I looked down at the table below. Shining silver, sparkling crystal, and fresh flowers. A setting fit for kings and queens.

"Up here are our guest rooms," Abel said. "We often have friends staying with us, friends from here in Bellis and also friends from other worlds."

He opened a door that led off the balcony. "Here, Michael, I would like you to take this room. You can have a shower and I'm sure you would like a change of clothes. The closet is full of new clothing. I don't think you'll have a problem finding something that fits."

"Abel, I don't know what to say. Thank you. Thank you so much."

"My pleasure," he said. "Well, I'm going to get changed myself. Our guests will be arriving soon, so when you're ready come on down and we'll have a big dinner together. It'll be fun." He made his way back down the stairs, and I stepped into my room.

Centred on one wall was a king size bed with brightly coloured bedding and six white pillows with gold edging. A bed. So people did have the need to sleep in heaven, or at least lie down and rest. The floor was carpeted, thick and luxurious. Soft, comfortable furniture was arranged on one side of the room, along with a carved and polished writing desk and chair. The opposite wall was made up of tall narrow doors extending from one corner to the other. I crossed the room and opened one of the doors. It was the closet that Abel had been talking about, full of clothing of all styles, colours, and sizes.

On the other wall was an arched doorway with double doors. I walked over and opened them. They both slid sideways and disappeared into the wall on either side. I stepped into the shower room. The floor and the walls were marble, and the shower was an open alcove that appeared to be cut out of natural rock, dark grey in colour and veined with blue and red. At the entrance to the shower, a pair of towels and a bathrobe hung beside two gold handles.

I had to try this out. I turned both handles about half way and water began to pour out of the rock high up in the roof. It flowed from above the rock like a waterfall, but when it had fallen less than half-way down, the water broke up into a heavy rain. I took a step forward and reached for the water. The temperature was perfect.

I quickly stripped off my clothes and stepped into the descending water. It felt good, as if I was standing in a rain forest during a tropical storm. I closed my eyes and enjoyed the experience. After a little while, my thoughts turned to dinner. Reluctantly, I turned off the water, dried myself with a thick towel, and wrapped the soft robe around me.

I walked over to the closet and checked out the clothing that hung there. There was plenty to choose from, but I wasn't sure what I should wear. How should I dress for dinner? Having an idea, I walked over to the door. Not wanting anyone to see me in a bathrobe, I opened it no more than a crack, and peered out. Down in the great dining room, I could see that a few guests had arrived. I was relieved that they all appeared to be dressed casually.

I closed the door and walked back to the closet. I picked out a beige pair of trousers of a cheesecloth-type material. They fit perfectly. Next, a cream button-up shirt with short sleeves followed by a cream lightweight wool sweater with a V neck. Finally, I selected a pair of canvas shoes that were extremely comfortable yet felt like they would also be good walking shoes.

I looked around the room and, satisfied that everything was in order, headed for the door.

CHAPTER 7

DINNER TIME

I stepped out onto the balcony and surveyed the room below. About thirty guests had arrived. Some were standing and talking among themselves, others were sitting in easy chairs that lined the wall down one side. About halfway down the other side of the room, several people, who I assumed to be musicians, were setting up their instruments. In addition, there were a few people moving back and forth from the direction of the kitchen. They would fiddle with something on the table for a moment, then disappear.

I walked around the balcony to the stairs and made my

| Old Dogs, Children, and Watermelon Wine |

way down. On reaching the bottom, I saw Abel making his way toward me, a woman at his side.

"Monica," he said, "this is Michael. He'll be joining us for dinner."

"Wonderful." Monica said. "Please go and meet our guests and let us know if there's anything you need."

I thanked them both and they moved away to speak with some other guests.

More people were arriving, and the musicians began to play. Piano, guitars, violin, and drums. They were joined by a female vocalist with one of the purest voices I'd ever heard. The music got the attention of the guests, and a few of them moved to an open area beside the band and began to dance.

An elderly gentleman was heading in my direction. He stopped in front of me. "You must be Michael."

I was a little surprised that he knew my name. "Yes, how did you know?"

"Oh, news travels fast around here. Tell me, where are you from?"

I had to give this some thought. "Well, I haven't been here long, I'm just travelling around. I suppose I'll have to settle down somewhere sooner or later."

"You don't need to be in any hurry to do that," he said. "One thing we have here is time, plenty of time, time to do whatever we want to do and take as much time as we want doing it."

"And you," I asked, "do you live close by? And what is it that you spend your time doing?"

"I live just a little way up the valley. I spend some time helping John in the orchards and quite a bit of time training the horses. Other than that, I'm either out fishing or walking with the dogs."

"A horse trainer, that's interesting. What are the horses trained for?"

"Parades and festivals and the like. There's nothing like horses when it comes to putting on a show. There's no better spectacle than a team of trained horses, all dressed up, circling an arena, each one perfectly in step with the other."

There was more I wanted to ask him, but we were interrupted by a loud clapping of hands and saw that Abel was attempting to get everyone's attention. "Please, everyone!" he shouted. "Take a seat at the table. We're about ready to eat."

Rufus, the man I'd been talking to, and I made our way over to the table and sat down. In moments others were sitting beside me and across the table from me, and introductions were made. I knew none of these people, yet somehow most of them knew my name.

Abel called out again. "Somebody say grace."

A man stood up and, in a loud voice, thanked God for the food, then sat down. I thought grace had been said, but someone else jumped up and gave thanks for the ripening fruit and the recent rain. People continued to rise from their seats and give thanks for something, and whatever it was, it was all good. The prayers flowed out,

| Old Dogs, Children, and Watermelon Wine |

one after the other, and my thoughts went back to Lucas and his lengthy thanksgiving. I was relieved he wasn't here to delay dinner any further. Eventually, the last amen was said and the chatter around the table resumed.

The musicians set their instruments aside and took their places at the table. Clearly they were not a hired band, but guests of the party here to entertain us. As they seated themselves, people appeared from the direction of the kitchen and began placing bowls and platters down the centre of the table. Bowls of crisp lettuce, platters of shrimp and smoked salmon, sliced tomatoes, cucumber, red onion, and baskets of bread. The servers left the room. But no one made a move for the food. In moments they were back carrying pitchers of wine, which they placed on the table with the food. One was a rich dark red in colour. The other clear, light, and tinted slightly pink. It looked somewhat familiar.

The servers took their seats. Like the musicians they were guests of the party. Friends and neighbours, who were helping out with the preparation and serving of dinner.

With everyone seated, we were ready to eat. I took a little of everything and placed it on the plate in front of me.

"Don't overdo it," a lady opposite me said. "This is just the appetizer. Would anyone like wine? Michael?"

I eyed the pink wine. "Tell me, what kind of wine is that?"

The lady turned to the man sitting beside her. "Stephen, what kind of wine is this?"

"Watermelon," he replied. "Its wonderful. Got it from Celosia when I was visiting there a little while ago,"

"Celosia," I said. "You didn't by any chance get it from a man by the name of Lucas, did you?"

Stephen looked surprised. "How did you know that?"

"I've tasted his wine before, and I have to tell you, I'd love to try it again."

The lady poured some wine into my glass, and I took a sip. Yes, that was it. Watermelon wine.

We ate, we drank, we laughed, we talked. Everyone was interested in what everyone else had been doing, was doing, and was going to be doing. No one was living a dull life, no one was lacking for things to do. Everyone was busy and happy to be so. I listened as people spoke of their experiences and adventures. Stories of being at huge gatherings, absolute bonanzas of feast and fellowship. Hundreds of thousands of people in one place at one time, worship and praise gatherings of crazy proportions. Music and dancing. I listened to stories of times when the Master himself had shown up at these events, and how he would reach out to every single individual in attendance. A seemingly impossible task.

The appetizers were about finished, and the servers moved around removing used plates and replacing them with clean ones.

Conversations continued, wine was sipped. Before long the workers were back, and many covered bowls were placed on the table in front of us. Once again we waited until everyone was seated. It was then that the lids were removed from the bowls.

I peered into the bowl directly in front of me and savoured the aroma. Wild game in a rich gravy with dumplings. Beside it a dish of potatoes, roasted to a golden brown. Dishes of colourful vegetables completed this fine dinner.

As I was eating, I recalled that I had eaten meals such as this before. Meat, potatoes, and vegetables. But here, in this place, in this world, with these people, food had never tasted so good.

I continued to listen to the conversations around me, conversations that included me, and I felt at home. I heard someone talking excitedly about "the game," obviously someone who had been to "the game." When the opportunity presented itself, I intended to find out more about this game he was talking about.

My empty plate was taken away, but we were not done yet. Platters of fruit were lined up on the table, honeydew melon cut into generous wedges, grapes, peaches, strawberries, and much more. It was a ripe and colourful display.

The pianist made his way over to the piano and sat down. As if passing time while waiting for the other musicians, he quietly played the blues.

Up and down the table, conversations intensified and the laughter became louder. Most of the fruit was gone but the wine was still flowing. The musicians returned to their instruments. We had a party.

After a some dancing and a little more wine, a tiredness came upon me, something I had not felt for quite some time. I spotted Abel on the other side of the room and made my way over to him.

"Abel," I said. "What a wonderful dinner and what wonderful people. I can't thank you enough."

"Good, good. So happy you could join us."

"Abel, what with the food and the wine and the dancing, I've come over rather tired. Would you mind if I went up to my room and rested for a while?"

"Please do," he replied. "Rest for as long as you wish. Much more dancing, and I'll be ready to sleep myself."

Sleep. I couldn't remember the last time I slept, so I was relieved to discover that sleeping was a heavenly function.

I made my way across the room to the stairs and ascended to the balcony. Looking back down into the great room, it seemed that a few people had left. Many of those who remained didn't look as if they intended to leave any time soon. They were talking, laughing, dancing, and sipping wine, the rich dark red along with my favourite, watermelon. Watermelon wine.

I opened the door to my room and walked over to the bed. I undressed and eased myself between the sheets. The bed was soft, warm, and comfortable. The light in the room was dim, and I could barely hear the music from below.

I lay there looking up at the ceiling. It was painted, intricate and decorative. Gold, purple, red, and cream. Then it was gone.

CHAPTER 8

BACK TO SCHOOL

I looked around the room at the hand painted ceiling and my clothes, folded on the chair beside the bed. Light was flooding in from the window. It was quiet. The music had stopped. I didn't know for how long I'd slept, and I didn't think it mattered.

I felt energized but the bed was comfortable and I was reluctant to leave it. Through the window I could see out into the universe, a universe held up in a cloudless sky. Comfortable as I was, I felt the need to make a move. I stood at the window and took in the whole panorama. Stars, planets, worlds, clearly visible in the light of day, no darkness in sight, only light and life.

But as I slept had it become dark? Had night fallen? Had I slept through a night and was it now morning? Was there night-time that separated one day from another? If so, how long did it last? How long was a day?

I had the feeling that perhaps I would never have all the answers to all the questions. Maybe some questions didn't have an answer. When it came to time, I was beginning to wonder if it existed at all in this world. How far was it to the city? How long would it take me to get to the next world? These were questions that I intended to ask, but I suspected that the answers given would likely tell me very little.

Beneath the sky, I surveyed the farmland. To one side, the orchards; to the other, fields of oats. Straight ahead of me was the vineyard, well-tended vines that reached to the highway.

The highway. I should get back on the road. It was a big universe. I should keep moving. I'd heard people at dinner talking about the city and had decided that was where I was headed.

I got dressed in my new clothes, made sure the room was somewhat tidy, then stepped out onto the balcony. The dining room below was empty. The party was over, as I had expected it would be. I made my way down the stairs and walked the length of the room. I noted that everything had been cleaned and polished. All was as it had been when I'd first entered. Everything was in its place and ready for the next dinner party.

I left the great room and walked across the wide hall, looking for any sign of life. A familiar smell steered me in the right direction. I stepped through an open door, and there sitting at the kitchen table was Abel and Monica. It was then I discovered the source of the aroma. They were drinking coffee.

"I hope you had a good rest," Abel said.

"I certainly did," I replied. "A very comfortable room, and what a view."

Monica placed a mug in front of me, and I took a sip. It was coffee alright, coffee as good as it gets. She moved across the kitchen and started slicing a loaf of bread.

"So Michael where are you heading for?" Abel asked. "You're welcome to stay with us longer, if you wish."

"Thank you, but no. I would like to go to the city. How long will it take me to get there?"

Abel looked at Monica. "You often go to the city Monica; how long does it take?"

Monica appeared to be deep in thought. "How long does it take to get to the city?" she said, half to herself. "Hmm . . . I'm not sure. If I stop for a visit on the way, it can take quite a while. If I don't stop at all, I get there much sooner."

Just as I suspected, time had no meaning, no value. I thought about asking how far it was to the city but decided against it. I'm sure nobody knows, I'm sure its never been measured. I supposed there would be no reason to. Time and distance had no place in this world.

"I'm heading back to the vineyard, Michael," Abel said. "Walk with me on your way back to the highway."

Monica came over to the table and handed me a small backpack. "Something for the journey," she said. I thanked her, we said our goodbyes, and Abel and I left the mansion. We walked across the coloured gravel, through the archway, and before long we were in the vineyard.

On arriving at the place where Abel needed to resume work, I turned to him and extended my hand. He shook it warmly, and I thanked him for his hospitality.

"Be sure to stop by and see us again," he said. "Anytime."

"To get to the city, do I continue on in the direction I was going?" I asked.

"Yes, this highway will take you straight there."

"And what is this city called?"

"Gaura," he said. "The city of Gaura."

Back on the highway, I walked at a steady pace, looking at everything around me. Farmland as far as I could see reached out to the low hills that served as the outer walls of the valley. I came to an orchard of plum trees, yellow plums, and I saw the pickup truck that I'd seen before; John's truck. My eyes searched the orchard, and after a while I spotted John some distance away. He gave me a wave, but we were too far from each other for any conversation.

I continued on, my eyes fixed on the horizon, and before long I saw what I was looking for. The skyline slowly took on a different shape and form. Buildings, many of them, spreading out wider and wider the closer

I got. It must be the city of Gaura.

As I neared the city, a few vehicles drove by, and a couple of people stopped and asked if I needed a ride. This world must be a hitchhikers dream. All a person would have to do is step out onto the highway, and in no time at all someone would drive up and offer to take them wherever they wanted to go.

On approaching the city limits, I passed a few buildings set back from the highway. They were spaced well apart, tidy and uncluttered. They were attractive structures but clearly not homes or residences. The land around each building was nicely landscaped with shrubs and flowers and large areas of lawn. Each building boasted a handsome entrance with stone pillars and a paved driveway.

I observed a few people standing outside the buildings. They had the appearance of men and women who perhaps worked there, but none of them seemed to be in any hurry to do anything. They gave the impression that their lives were pleasing, unhurried, and comfortable.

One building in particular interested me. As I was trying to figure out what it might be, I noticed a bench on the opposite side of the road, the kind of bench that might be placed in a park or rest area. I walked over, put my backpack on the bench, and sat down beside it.

I watched the building. It was quiet. There was no one in sight. No sign of life.

I reached into my backpack and took out a paper bag and a bottle of fruit juice. I removed a thick sandwich from

| Old Dogs, Children, and Watermelon Wine |

the bag and took a bite. Turkey, lettuce, and tomato with blackcurrant jelly. It tasted really good. "Thanks Monica."

The building across the street had a primary level above a raised basement. It was long and wide, with stone steps providing access to the double-wide front doors. Large windows were set close together and circled the entire building. The roof was steeply pitched with several skylights that suggested vaulted ceilings or perhaps a loft area.

The building was in the middle of a field of closely mown grass that extended well beyond the building, with wide strips on both sides. At the back was a sports area with goal posts for soccer, football, field hockey, and more. Down each side there were climbing frames, slides, swings, all kinds of recreational equipment. At the front, dozens of picnic tables were scattered around, reaching up to the sturdy but decorative fence that separated the property from the road.

The silence was broken by the ringing of a bell. It lasted for a few seconds, then it was silent again. But not for long. All of a sudden, the front doors of the building burst open, and children started pouring down the steps and overflowed out onto the grass. Children aged around five to ten years old, dressed in uniform, white shirts with grey shorts or skirts. They kept coming, two hundred, three hundred of them. The stream of little bodies was not diminishing. Five, maybe six hundred, all jostling for position, each one trying to get ahead of the other. It was as if someone had opened the door to a closet full of ping-pong balls.

The children separated into groups of varying sizes and made their way to different areas of the field. Some to the sports field at the back, some to the swings and slides, others sat at the picnic tables and opened up their lunch boxes. A few adults were wandering around, some with mugs in their hands. School teachers, I presumed, taking a break along with the children.

Schools in heaven. It was something I had never given thought to. I had wondered, though, if there would be children in heaven. Of course, I knew that children went to heaven. But then what? Did they grow up to be adults, or did they remain children? And were children born in heaven?

I watched them from across the street, a thousand kids, and tried to imagine a heaven that was adults only. Grown-ups and no children. No children would mean no schools, no playgrounds, no toys, no hide-and- seek or hopscotch. Without children, there would be no energy, no growth, no new life.

I watched those little people, eating, playing, laughing, and I wondered what the future held for them. Surely they would grow, get older, and mature. Surely they would go out into this universe and find their world, discover their purpose, and assume the role that the Master had for them.

I finished my sandwich and juice and sat watching and listening to the hum of activity across the street. Then the school bell rang again, and the children started to make their way toward the front steps. Moving slower than when they exited the building, they climbed the steps and disappeared inside. With no one remaining outside, it was quiet once again.

I stood and picked up my backpack. It was time to head into the city.

CHAPTER 9

CITY LIFE

I reached the city gates, but there were no gates, only a pair of towering pillars built from steel, rock, and glass. No gates. It would seem that, in this world, containment was not required. People were free to come and go as they pleased. At the entrance, the road forked left and right, diverting traffic around the city. Clearly, motorized vehicles did not use the city streets.

I walked between the pillars and I was in the city, surrounded by buildings built from rock and stone of varying texture and colour. The windows and doors of each building were painted differently, every colour from midnight blue to brilliant white. None of the buildings were more than three stories high. There were no skyscrapers in sight.

I walked slowly, looking from one side to the other, and sensed that the surface I was walking on had changed. It had a different feel compared to walking on the highway. I looked down and examined the road's surface. Its colour was a soft yellow that seemed to have a glow to it, and it had the appearance of being warm. It looked like . . . No, it couldn't be.

I walked on, paying attention to the activity on the street. There were hundreds of people, yet room enough for everyone. In the buildings on both sides of the street, people seemed to be doing business of some kind. I stopped and watched. People would leave the street, enter a building, and after a short time would come back out carrying a bag they hadn't had before. They were not doing anything out of the ordinary. They were doing what everyone did in the city. They were shopping.

What had I expected of heaven? Had I expected that there would be no shops, no farms, no cars, no dinner parties, no children, no watermelon wine? Had I expected to be just floating around on a cloud for eternity, without purpose, without reason?

I watched a man and a woman coming out of a shop carrying a large bag, and suddenly realized that sooner or later I would need to buy things myself. Food, shoes, get a haircut. Then it hit me, I didn't have any money.

Without it, how would I be able to get the things I needed? These thoughts worried me a little as I continued on up the street.

Seeing that the doors to one of the shops were fixed open, I moved into a position that allowed me to look inside. The walls were stacked with shoes and hats, and there were rails loaded with men's and women's clothing. What I assumed to be a shop assistant was helping a couple pick out an item.

As I watched them, a man walked by me and went into the shop. He walked slowly down the side wall and tried on a couple of hats. He found one he liked, kept it on, and made his way back to the front door. When he passed the assistant, he touched his hat, smiled, and said, "Thank you." Then he left the building.

Back inside, the couple had found what they were looking for, and the assistant placed their purchases in a bag. Then, like the man with the hat, they headed out the door and made their way lazily up the street.

I didn't see these people pay for anything; they just got what they wanted and left, without any money changing hands. Perhaps they had an account there and were sent a bill. That was the only explanation I could think of.

I carried on up the street, passing shops and stores displaying everything from fresh vegetables to bicycles. I came upon a library and could not resist stepping inside. Slowly, I walked the aisles. Books, tens of thousands of them. I was not looking for anything in particular, but there were a few titles that I was familiar with. Aisle after aisle, solid walls of books. I could easily have spent a good part of eternity right here.

Back on the street, my progress was halted once again, this time by an art gallery. I lingered a while to admire oil paintings, water-colours, and pencil drawings. Figures carved from wood and others formed in rock. All of it the work of gifted artists.

On the street again, I passed a number of cafes and restaurants with people sitting at tables inside and out. They were enjoying bowls of salad and sandwiches, tall glasses of fruit juice, and mugs of coffee and tea. I found an empty table and sat down.

I watched the street, the people, some in groups of three or four, some in pairs, others on their own. Some moved along at a leisurely pace, others stood and chatted. It seemed that a lot of people knew a lot of people, and if someone didn't know someone they were soon introduced. People sat at tables eating and drinking, others studied the goods in shop windows. Shopkeepers who were not tending to customers sat in chairs beside their front door.

I looked at the faces of the people around me and saw features and skin colouring that revealed the origins of many nations. As I watched them, it was clear that they were now all of one nation.

A little woman walking up the middle of the street claimed my attention. She wore a knitted hat, more of a bonnet really, and had on a thick cardigan buttoned up to her chin. Her heavy skirt was long and reached almost all the way down to a pair of shoes that looked like they would last forever. She carried a bag in each hand.

When she reached my position, she stopped and looked around. Then, uninvited, she sat down at my table. She seemed a little flustered as she rummaged around in her bags. She took items out and placed them on the table, then replaced them in the bags. There were several empty tables around us, but it seemed perfectly normal for her to take a seat at mine.

Eventually, she appeared to be satisfied that everything was in order. She placed her bags on the ground beside her, looked at me, and said, "Hello, I'm Ruthie."

"Michael," I replied. "I see you're doing a little shopping."

"Yes, yes. Needed to pick up some necessities, and of course, the odd little luxury."

I felt comfortable talking to this woman, as if we had immediately developed a friendship. "Luxury," I said. "Can I see?"

She reached into one of her bags, removed a bottle, and passed it to me. "Its made in another world," she said. "Celosia. Its not known to be made anywhere else."

It was a clear glass bottle with a label attached to it, but I had no need to study the label. Through the glass I saw a clear liquid. Clear, but with a faint touch of pink. Watermelon wine. "I've tasted this before, Ruthie, and you're right, it's a luxury."

| Old Dogs, Children, and Watermelon Wine |

A young woman emerged from a small cafe close to our table. She was carrying two cups, each one on a saucer. She came over to our table and placed the cups in front of us.

"I think you'll enjoy this," she said. She gave us a smile and walked back into the cafe.

Ruthie picked up her cup and took a sip. "Tea," she said. "It's flavoured with something, I'm not quite sure what. Tastes good though." She looked at me. "Are you going to try it?"

I was not sure what I should do. "Ruthie, I have a bit of a problem. I don't have any money to pay for it."

She looked at me with a somewhat serious expression, and for a few moments I felt like I really did have a problem. Then she burst out laughing.

"Neither do I," she said, and laughed again. Not knowing what to say or do, I took a sip of tea. I was not much of a tea drinker, but this tea I could get used to. Like Ruthie, I was unable to identify the flavour, an herb of some kind.

Ruthie seemed to be over whatever it was that had amused her. "You haven't been here very long, have you?"

"I'm not sure exactly how long I've been here," I replied, "but you're right, it hasn't been very long."

"Okay. I'll explain a few things to you. You don't need money. We have no need for money, not in this world, not in any world. That's the way God designed things."

I was a little mystified. "Are you telling me I can just walk into any of these shops or stores, take whatever I need, and pay nothing?" I pointed down the street. "Are you saying that I could go into that shop and leave with a bag of apples? And that one, go in and walk out in a pair of new shoes? How about the bicycle store? Could I go in there and take any bicycle I want? Can I have all these things without having to pay for them?"

"It's really quite simple," she replied. "When a farmer needs new clothes, he goes to the people who make clothes and takes what he needs. He doesn't have to pay anything; there is no charge. When the clothes maker needs food, he goes to the farmer and takes all the food he needs. He doesn't have to pay anything; there is no charge. When a builder builds a house for a school teacher, he doesn't present a bill. The school teacher educates the builder's children, and there are no school fees."

She paused and looked at me for a moment, "Are you beginning to understand how the Master has figured things out for us?"

I nodded. "I think so."

"Everyone has their place here. We all have a purpose, a role to fulfill. Each one of us has a job, if you like."

She seemed to be finished saying what she wanted to say, so I asked her. "What's your purpose, Ruthie? What's your job?"

"Bees," she said. "I put hives in farmers' orchards; I jar the honey, bring it into the city, and give it to the shopkeepers." She pointed across the street. "That little shop over there, they have my honey if you want some."

"It sounds like the perfect way to do business," I said. "You come into town with jars of honey and leave with watermelon wine. Brilliant."

We both sat for a while and sipped our tea. I wondered if this way of doing business could be flawed in any way. "Does anyone ever take advantage?" I asked. "I mean, are there any greedy people, people who take more than they need, leaving others short of what they need? Are there lazy people who don't work, yet take advantage of what others have worked for?"

"It may seem hard to believe," she replied, "but there are no greedy people, and there are no lazy people. There's not even any sick people. Everyone does their job, and they're happy doing it. With each of us fulfilling our role, we always have more than enough for our needs. What we don't have here in Gaura we can easily get from another city, or even another world. Like the watermelon wine."

The tea was finished, and I leaned back in my chair. I watched the people around me and realized that I had to become like them. I needed to find my place, go to work, and fulfill my purpose, "Ruthie, I need to settle somewhere, get a job, become useful. I can't spend eternity just wandering around the universe."

"You won't," she replied. "You'll find your world, your purpose, but you have to wait for the Master's instructions,"

"When will that be?"

"When you're ready. Could be any time."

"How will I know that the instructions I get are from the Master himself?"

"You will know."

"How did you get your instructions, how did it come about that you're a beekeeper?"

Ruthie looked away into the distance as if recalling an event from the past. "I was not far from here, just a little beyond the city limits, walking the highway, just as you're doing, going nowhere in particular, just enjoying the walk. I came to an apple orchard. It was in full blossom, pink and white, absolutely beautiful, and the fragrance was... heavenly." She let out a little laugh. "Well it would be, wouldn't it? Anyway, in the orchard I saw a row of bee hives, twenty or thirty of them, and there was a man out there. He seemed to be checking the hives, tending to them in some way. For some reason, I suddenly developed a fascination for bees and honey, and had to take a closer look. So, I stepped into the orchard and made my way toward the hives. As I approached, the man looked up and said... Ah, good. I was beginning to wonder when you were going to get here."

Ruthie paused, giving me a chance to speak. "This man, he was expecting you?"

"So it seemed. He told me how delighted he was that I was there to care for the hives and collect the honey. He told me what a wonderful job I would do, and that he would stop by and see me whenever he was passing. Then he told me he needed to move on, said he had work

| Old Dogs, Children, and Watermelon Wine |

to do in the next world but would never be far away if I needed him."

Again, she focused on something in the distance.

"So it was him," I said.

"No doubt about it. It was him."

"Did you say anything to him?"

"I think I said something like, I'll do my best, and thanks for everything. What was I supposed to say to the Master of the universe? Whatever it was I said, he placed his hand on my shoulder and smiled. Then he turned and walked up to the highway. When he reached the road, he headed toward the city and was soon out of sight."

"And has he since stopped by to see you?"

"He has indeed, but I'm not going to relate those times to you. The company of this man must be experienced first-hand. Your time will come."

The girl from the cafe came back out and picked up our empty cups. "Did you enjoy the tea?" she asked.

"Very much," Ruthie replied.

"It's flavoured with some kind of herb," I said. "Can you tell me what it is?"

"Shiso," she said. "Good isn't it?" She smiled again, then disappeared back inside the cafe.

Ruthie reached for her bags and stood up. "Time for me to go, Michael."

"Goodbye Ruthie." She stepped in close to me, bent slightly at the waist, and kissed the top of my head.

I watched her as she made her way up the street. A delightful little lady in her bonnet, long skirt, and sensible shoes.

It was time for me to make a move as well. I stood, hooked my backpack over my shoulders, and headed up the street, passing many stores, shops, and galleries. Temporary structures had been erected and lined the centre of the street. They were no more than small tents, stocked with fruit and cut flowers. Others offered ice cream and chocolate. There were numerous street musicians; when one was out of earshot, there would be another. People would stop, eat chocolate and ice cream, and enjoy the music. Everything from rock 'n' roll to the classics. I made my way slowly, stopping frequently.

After seeing much and walking far, I saw ahead of me two pillars built of steel, rock, and glass, identical to those I had passed through when entering the city. Beyond the pillars, the city gave way to open countryside and farmland. The soft yellow of the city street returned to asphalt pavement.

I was leaving the city of Gaura.

CHAPTER 10

ONE OVER PAR

Back on the highway saw the return of motorized vehicles. I passed a large parking area, there for those motorists who wished to walk into the city. Again, there were buildings outside the city limits, spaced out and nicely maintained, giving the impression of being places of work. The outside appearance gave no indication of what went on inside. Perhaps in one clothing was made, and in another food prepared. I thought about investigating, but decided against it.

I moved on, leaving the city and its suburbs behind. As I walked, it became warmer, hot even. As if knowing that a little shade would be welcome, the highway took me into an avenue of trees. Trees of varying species, tall and leafy, overhanging the highway on both sides. I enjoyed the relief and shelter they offered.

Through the trees to my right was a huge lawn, a wide strip of grass, dark green and closely mown. I made my way through the trees and stood at the tree line. The grass was like a fine carpet, almost too good to walk on, a runway of green with trees also lining the opposite side about fifty paces away. To the right and about two hundred paces away, I observed a small area of grass slightly elevated from the ground around it. Turning in the other direction, I saw a gently undulating area of lighter green, somewhat circular in shape and about thirty steps across. Offset from its centre, a short thin pole with a flag on top stood fixed in the ground.

There are people, I'm sure, who would do everything that was required of them to get to heaven for this and this alone. A golf course.

I heard voices in the distance. Back down the fairway I saw two men stepping up onto the elevated tee box. They set their golf bags down, and one of them prepared to hit his drive. He grabbed his driver, teed his ball up, and took a couple of practice swings. Satisfied that he was ready, he stepped up to his ball, assumed a solid stance, and made a nice smooth swing. The ball rose into the air, landed a little way past where I was standing, and came to rest in the middle of the fairway. Perfect. The second

| Old Dogs, Children, and Watermelon Wine |

golfer hit his drive and achieved a similar result. These guys could play.

As they made their way up the fairway, I took a few steps back into the trees. I didn't want them to see that I was watching.

The player who hit the second drive got to his ball first. He considered the shot for a few moments, pulled out a club, and took dead aim at the flag. He got the ball into the air nicely, but it faded away to the right. I saw it catch the branch of a tree and drop down into the rough grass, short and right of the green.

The golfer with the slightly longer drive stepped in and addressed his ball. He too hit it high, and it landed on the left edge of the green. It looked as if he had a birdie putt coming up, but the ball was still moving. I heard shouts of, "Hang on! Hang on!" But the slope took over, and the ball rolled off the green and down into a low area, leaving a tricky chip back up to the putting surface.

I had to smile, because now I knew. God gave us no more help on the golf course in heaven than he did on the golf course on Earth.

I watched the players complete the hole. A pair of bogey fives. Not bad. Could have been worse.

I returned to the highway. As I continued down the shaded avenue, I detected movement above me and looked up. Perched side by side on a branch were two birds about the size of magpies. They were steel blue in colour, the top of their heads yellow, and their wings edged in red.

Simple colouring, uncomplicated, yet they made a striking pair. I watched them as they watched me.

I moved on slowly and heard them leave their perch. They flew over top of me and settled in a tree a little way ahead. This went on for some time, and I was enjoying the company. One more time, they flew overhead, but this time they didn't wait for me. They flew on, down the avenue and out of sight. Maybe I'd catch up to them later.

As I walked, I gave thought to seeking out the ones I loved and finding my world. I wondered when I would receive my instructions from the Master. Then I rested on Ruthie's words. "Your time will come."

Up ahead something was lying beneath a tree, a small animal curled up and seemingly asleep. As I got closer, I saw that it was a dog, brown and white and of medium size. On hearing my footsteps, he slowly lifted his head and looked in my direction. He watched me for a moment before he stood up. He stretched and yawned, then walked to the roadside, where he sat and watched as I approached. It was as if he had been waiting for me, just taking a nap until I arrived. I stopped beside him.

"Hello boy, what are you doing here?" He remained sitting, but his tail moved from side to side as if sweeping the grass. I crouched down and held his head between my hands. His ears were soft, his coat fairly long, and he had a pointed nose. My favourite kind of dog. A border collie. He was not a puppy, an old dog I guessed. He showed no sign of wanting to run around, he just looked up at

| Old Dogs, Children, and Watermelon Wine |

me with his mouth open and his tongue out. His eyes indicated that he wouldn't mind at all just going back to his spot under the tree and resuming his nap.

I loved this dog, but I had to leave him and move on. "Well, old boy, I'd like to stay with you longer, but I have to go." I scratched his head a couple of times and stood up straight. He looked at me as if he didn't want me to leave. I wanted to take him with me, but I figured he belonged to someone, and they would surely be expecting him to return home soon. I turned my attention back to the highway and resumed walking. After a few paces, I stopped and looked back. He was watching me leave. "Good boy. Go on home now." What a great dog, I wished I could take him with me.

The avenue of trees came to an end, and I stepped out into the light of the universe. Some of the heat that I'd felt before was gone and the walk remained pleasant.

On both sides of the road, the farmland had returned. In the distance I could see machinery working in the field. I quickened my pace, anxious to get a closer look. It was a tractor, a big one. A John Deere. Four wheel drive with at least three hundred horsepower. It was pulling an eight-furrow plough. I watched the big green tractor move easily over the land, the plough opening up the soil and leaving a light cloud of dust in its wake.

As I watched, I felt something brush against my leg. I looked down and there he was, the border collie. He was looking up at me, his mouth open, his tongue hanging out, his tail slapping from side to side.

I crouched down in front of him. "What are you doing following me? I told you to go home." He looked away from me, and I was pretty sure he knew what I was talking about, but he wasn't going to admit it, even if he could.

I stood up and keeping my eyes on him, took two steps forward. The old dog was immediately at my side once again, looking up at me as if to say: "Come on then, lets get going."

Maybe he didn't belong to anyone. Maybe he was just waiting under that tree for someone to walk with.

"Okay, we'll walk together, but what should I call you? I don't know your name." I looked down at him and gave this some thought.

"How about . . . Bob?"

His ears straightened up and he tipped his head to one side. It was as if he'd heard a name he recognized, a name he was familiar with. Maybe he was just pleased with the name I'd given him.

"Okay, Bob it is. Lets go, Bob."

The two of us walked and walked, rested for a while, then walked again. Bob walked on the grass shoulder, I on the pavement. He was no trouble, and I enjoyed his company. The traffic was light, the universe was bright, and its warmth surrounded us.

We passed several roads that branched off from the main highway. Looking in the direction they were headed, I could see the skyline of the occasional town or city in the distance.

| Old Dogs, Children, and Watermelon Wine |

Across the farmland and beyond were rolling hills and dense forest. Towns, cities, farmland, and open countryside. None of which was unfamiliar to me, but in the light of this world, this universe, I felt like I was seeing creation for the first time.

After walking far, Bob and I came upon a small village. Single level buildings, which included a few shops and stores. Cheerful people walked the streets. They acknowledged me but mostly made a fuss of Bob.

We came to a small building, open at the front, with a counter extending from one side to the other. A woman appeared in the opening and called me over.

"You look as if you need something to eat," she said. She pointed at a small table. "Sit there, I'll prepare something for you."

I seated myself at the table and Bob lay down beside me. We were sitting on a small patio among a few other tables, most of which were occupied by people enjoying food and drinks and each other's company. The village had the feel of a small tourist town, no one in any hurry to go anywhere, no timeline to be met, no sense of urgency. I watched the people, my thoughts turning to the world from which they had come and the world they now occupied. What was their purpose? What was the role they were required to play?

My thoughts were interrupted by the nice lady placing a wooden platter in front of me. "I'll be right back," she said, before once again disappearing inside. Moments later she was back. "And something for . . ." She looked down.

"That's Bob," I said.

"Something for Bob."

Bob was on his feet like a shot. I'd never seen him move so fast. She had in her hand a large bone with a generous amount of meat on it. "There you go Bob," she said.

Bob took the bone carefully, gave the lady an appreciative look, and sauntered silently away, disappearing behind the building. Either he liked to eat alone, or maybe he was afraid someone might steal his meal.

"Enjoy your lunch," the woman said. "Both of you."

I told her how much I appreciated her kindness, then looked down at my plate. A miniature loaf of bread, a thick slice of cheese, pickled onions, a wedge of pork pie, a hard-boiled egg, and a whole tomato.

A ploughman's lunch. Well, I was in farming country.

I sat and worked my way through the food in front of me, enough to sustain me for some time to come. As I ate, I gave thought to those who had produced the food and the woman who had prepared it for me, and I wondered again what my purpose, my role, would be. Farmer, restaurateur, carpenter? Maybe a winemaker, like Lucas.

The busy lady set two platters on the table next to mine, then walked over and picked up my empty plate. "I hope that will keep you going for the remainder of your journey," she said.

"I'm sure it will keep me going for a long time," I replied. "Bob too. Thank you."

"Do you know where you're going?" she asked.

"I'm not sure. To the next world, but I don't know what or where that world is."

"Well, get back out on the highway and look at the worlds around you. You can pick any one of them; it's your choice. Keep looking. Eventually the Master will lead you to your world."

As I stood up and prepared to leave, she gave me a small package. "Something for your backpack," she said.

Back on the road, Bob and I, well satisfied after our big meal, continued on our way. After a while I realized there had been a change in our surroundings. No longer were there crops and orchards on either side of us. Looking back, I saw that we were leaving the farmland behind us. The meadows with coloured flowers were returning, and the horizon was void of city skylines. Nothing but painted fields that reached out to a fluorescent sky.

We had left the world of Bellis. A man and his dog, back on heaven's highway, between worlds.

CHAPTER 11
THE DARK

"So, Bob, we're on our way to the next world. This is your last chance if you want to change your mind. Do you want to go back, Bob? Do you want to go home?" He looked at me for a moment, then back at the road ahead and kept walking.

He'd given me his answer.

After a spell of walking, I stopped and looked back at the world we'd left behind. I no longer saw Bellis as a flat land mass, but as a mighty globe in its place in the universe. It appeared close, almost on top of us, but I knew we had traveled far from it, a distance that could not be measured.

| Old Dogs, Children, and Watermelon Wine |

I returned my attention to the highway ahead. As I walked, I studied the universe around me. Worlds surrounded by spheres of light, and stars of translucent colour. It was a universe that was alive and electrifying.

From time to time, we came to a road that led away from the main highway. A number of times, I stopped and looked down those roads. Each one seemed to point directly toward another world far in the distance.

I passed several such roads, and then came upon one that was unlike any of the others. Its width was that of only one vehicle. Looking down this narrow road, I could not determine where it may lead to. It disappeared after only a short distance and gave no indication of where it might take us.

At this junction in the road was a fallen tree that had been roughly carved into a bench, and I welcomed the opportunity to sit. Bob walked over to the shade of a nearby tree and lay down.

After resting for a while, I was ready to move on. I eyed the highway, but my attention returned to the little narrow road. It was not the direction in which I wanted to go, but I was curious to know its purpose, where and what it led to. I made up my mind. I'd take this new road, but I'd only go so far. Then I'd turn back and rejoin the highway.

I got up from the log. "Come on, Bob, time to go." Bob didn't make a move. He looked at me for a moment before lowering his head onto his front paws and closing his eyes.

I really didn't like leaving him, but I was not going far; I should be back before too long. "Okay, Bob, you wait here, I won't be long." He didn't seem at all concerned, so I got going.

Little changed from what I'd become accustomed to. The grass was green, the flowers bright, the universe vibrant.

The road appeared to be going nowhere, to have no purpose, and I thought about turning back. Then the surface beneath my feet changed. The pavement became uneven and cracked, the asphalt broken. After only a few more steps, it had become coarse gravel. Perhaps the end of the road was not far away. So, I continued on.

Walking became more difficult in the gravel, and I knew that before much longer I would be turning back. The atmosphere had cooled, and the universe around me had lost some of its radiance. There was no reason why I would go any farther, but I felt drawn forward, needing to know what lay ahead.

It became cold and was getting darker. It was as if night was coming, but the cold and the darkness had an unnatural feel, a presence that was out of place in a universe I was becoming familiar with. The stars were barely visible, dark sinister shapes that were beginning to blend into the darkness around them. It was becoming increasingly difficult to see the road ahead, and I stumbled on the uneven surface.

Without stopping, I unhooked my backpack, pulled out my sweater, and slipped it over my head.

Turning around and going back should have been easy but, inexplicably, I was unable to. My mind returned to the crossing of the river, how any effort to turn back only took me deeper. I remembered, too, coming out on the other side and entering a glorious universe. I felt sure that would not be the case this time.

My feet became heavy, and my pace slowed. Something wanted to push me ahead, but my feet were fixed firmly to the ground, and I was thankful for the restraint. I strained to take one more step forward, but to no avail. I was standing in total darkness, looking into total darkness.

I had the sense of standing on the edge of a precipice, a pit, out of which flowed darkness, a blackness that shut out everything around it. The planets, the stars, the worlds, the living universe was gone.

I looked into the darkness, and that was all I saw. A void, a world that could not be passed through, a world that did not lead to the light on the other side but led only to greater darkness. What was this dark world doing here, and what had brought me to it? What did the darkness hold? What was its purpose, and what was the extent of its power?

"They can see us, you know."

Startled, I turned my head, my eyes searching for the one who had spoken. But the darkness yielded nothing. I could see nothing, but the voice, a man's voice, was close. There was someone standing beside me.

"Who are you?" I tried to keep the fear out of my voice.

"My name is Marcus."

"What are you doing here? What do you want with me?"

"I followed you."

"You followed me? Why did you follow me?"

"I wanted to make sure you didn't go too far. Any farther and you may have been unable to return."

I was becoming less fearful. The voice carried authority, but was not unfriendly, so I continued my questioning. "Return from what? And who are they? You said, they can see us."

Marcus paused a few moments, as if giving thought to my questions before answering.

"Very few know what the darkness holds. I've walked within that dark world, and I've seen the misery, but no one knows the full extent of its horror. For those within it's their world. There's no way out."

We both became silent as I tried to envision living in a world of darkness, a world without light. Marcus spoke again.

"Being in there is not their greatest torment. What they see behind us is what torments them most. Turn around and see for yourself."

I turned away from the dark pit and saw what they could see. Far away through the blackness of this unnatural night, an invisible horizon reached as far as my vision allowed. It was ablaze with light, light that had colour and movement, light that was alive. A living universe.

"That is what they see," Marcus said. "The worlds they want but can never reach. Living in their world, that light is all they can see. So they watch it. They watch the light, while at the same time knowing that the walls of darkness that restrain them will never come down."

As if sensing that I was about to turn around, Marcus said, "Don't look back. Look ahead to the light. That's our world. We don't belong here."

There was more I needed to know. "Those people back there, trapped in a world of despair, a world of horror and without light, how did they get there? What did they do to deserve being in such a place?"

Marcus allowed a few moments to pass. "They made the wrong choices."

In the silence that followed, I considered his response. "We must go." he said finally.

I attempted to take a step forward, and my feet moved easily. Keeping my eyes upon the lighted horizon, I walked toward it. The sound of footsteps on gravel assured me that Marcus was at my side. Somehow managing not to stumble in the darkness, we made our way through the night in silence. I was anxious to return to the light and the warmth.

Through the darkness I saw a circular outline ahead of us. It was barely visible, appearing as black on black. As we moved forward, another began to materialize, as if a pale light was being painted on its circumference. Slowly, the globe took on full light and one by one, others joined it.

When the road ahead became visible, I turned my head and saw my companion for the first time.

Marcus was a tall, thin black man. He was wearing a light-coloured suit, casual and loose fitting. There was grey hair at his temple below a straw hat. He towered above me, an old man, yet he had a powerful frame, and his posture was upright. On this uneven and rocky road, his stride did not falter. His gaze remained fixed ahead, and we walked in silence.

The universe was back, fully alight, fully alive, and we left the gravel and returned to the little paved road. The grass was green, the flowers bright, and I heard the sound of running water nearby. The dark world from which I'd come now seemed far away.

Up ahead, the main highway came into sight. I saw the little log bench, and there under the tree was good old Bob, still lying in the same spot. He watched us as we made our way up the narrow road. Upon reaching the bench, Marcus and I both sat. Bob came over, stood in front of me, and looked me up and down as if checking me over. I wondered why he'd not wanted to go with me down the narrow road. Perhaps he knew it led to a place he didn't want to go, a place he feared. He would have been right.

Marcus looked at Bob but was clearly not inclined to make a fuss of him. "Is this your dog?" he asked.

"Well, we've been travelling together for some time now, so yes, I guess I can call him mine."

"He was sitting under that tree when I turned off the highway to follow you. He looked as if he was waiting for someone."

There was much more I wanted to ask this man. "How often do you do this, Marcus, follow people down this road?"

"I watch as much as I can. When someone ventures down there, I follow them. Most of them don't get far. When the road gets rough, they turn back. Like you, a few are drawn forward all the way to the edge of the dark pit, and I make every effort to reach them before they go any farther."

"Do any of them get any farther?"

"Everyone I've reached has turned back, but I don't know how many I've missed or how many I've been unable to reach."

"You said you'd walked within the dark world. Were you able to see anything at all?"

"I saw dark figures moving around, barely visible. When they turned toward the light, I glimpsed their faces, but for a fleeting moment only. It was as if they looked at me, then immediately turned away. Like walking past a mirror in the dark; a sudden reflective movement that's gone in an instant."

Marcus paused again, reliving experiences past. "What I saw in that fraction of time was something I hope never to see again."

I gazed into the distance and tried to imagine living in such a world. "How did you make your escape?" I asked.

"If those within the dark world are trapped there, how is it you were able to leave?"

"Like you, I was curious. I wanted to know where the road led but, unlike you, when I reached the edge, I was not restrained. I walked into the pit itself. Once I experienced the horror within, I tried to leave but something was holding me back. I fought against it, but its grip was relentless. I was not going to give up the fight. I wasn't going to stay there; I couldn't. I was becoming exhausted and giving up hope when suddenly I broke free. No longer a captive, I walked away and didn't stop until I reached the light."

"How is it that others cannot leave, break free, as you did?"

Marcus momentarily looked down the narrow road. "I didn't belong there. That was not my place. That world could not hold me. Unlike those who are trapped there, I made the right choices; by making those choices, I was forever protected from the darkness."

I gazed into the universe around me and gave thought to the one who created it. I turned to the old man beside me, and again I pressed him for answers. "God, if he wanted to, could take those people out of the darkness and bring them into the light ... Couldn't he?"

Marcus did not reply, his eyes remained fixed on something far away.

Still, I pressed him further. "I mean, God can do anything, right? He could break down the walls of darkness and allow them to walk out into the light, into his universe. He could do that... Couldn't he?"

Again I was met with silence. "Do you think he will, Marcus? Do you think he'll set them free? You know he is able. You know he has the power to do all things. Will he release them?"

Marcus turned toward me, appearing hesitant to respond. Again he looked away into the distance before replying.

"Don't count on it."

CHAPTER 12

LOST IN THE SIXTIES

I watched the tall thin man make his way toward the horizon and wondered where I might be had he not shown up. His destination was in the opposite direction to mine, so we had parted company.

When he disappeared, I looked down the narrow road expecting to see in the distance, a dark cloud or some evidence of the dark world that existed there. But I saw only the universe, the heaven's, lit up and extending as far as the eye could see.

I turned my attention back to the highway. I, too, should move on. No longer cold, I pulled my sweater off and folded it into my backpack. As I did, I saw the package I'd been given in the village. I opened it and discovered the goodies inside. I took out a cookie, then returned the package to my pack.

Bob was at my side and seemed eager to get going. We resumed our journey, Bob walking on the grass, me on the pavement. Walking in the light and warmth, the dark world I'd left behind was becoming a distant memory.

Bob spotted something, and my eyes searched for what had caught his attention. Camouflaged against a grove of trees, a deer and fawn stood perfectly still, watching us. They made no attempt to move, and Bob let them be.

Before moving on, I looked back in the direction from which we had come. In the distance, a rapid flash of light caught my eye. Almost all the way back to the horizon was a vehicle heading in our direction. This was the first vehicle I'd seen for some time. We waited and watched as it made its way toward us.

As it got closer it began to take shape. It was more of a van than a car. A small bus-style vehicle, windows down the side, paint work of bright colours, and a flat front. No hood.

When it was close, I saw it all. Red, blue, pink, yellow, and more. Custom wide tyres, a lowered chassis, and the familiar rattle of the rear mounted engine. It was a Volkswagen van from the sixties.

The VW slowed, then came to a stop on the side of the road. Two young women and a young man stepped out of the brightly coloured van. The man had a full beard, and his hair reached down to his shoulders. He was wearing faded jeans, and the colours on his T-shirt competed well with the paintwork on the van. The hair of one of the girls hung down to her waist. She too was wearing jeans, with a pink shirt and a multi- coloured headband.

The last of the three wore shorts and a flowery blouse. She also had long hair, which was tied back in a ponytail. None of them were wearing shoes.

A bunch of hippies, driving heaven's highway in a Volkswagen van from the sixties.

"Hey, man, what's happening?" The young man strode toward me, grasped my hand in his, and pulled me into a solid hug. The girls were right behind him, and I got the same treatment from them. When they were finished with me, Bob also received a generous greeting, which he seemed to quite enjoy.

We introduced ourselves. They were Poppy, Lois, and Conrad. "Well, Mickey," I assumed Conrad was talking to me, "lets sit over there on the grass and get to know each other,"

Lois turned and walked back to the van. "I'll go get some water and see what I can find for us to eat," she said.

Conrad and I moved away from the highway and sat on the grass. Still with some disbelief, I stared at the old Volkswagen. Lois had the side door open and was moving stuff around. After a while she returned with an empty bag and empty water container.

"Are you coming Poppy?" she asked. The two of them, accompanied by Bob, disappeared through the trees. I had no idea where they were going with an empty bag and water bottle, but they seemed to know what they were doing.

Conrad turned to me, "So, Mickey, tell me what's going on, man. You're in between worlds here. You know that, don't you? Tell me where you've been and where you're going."

I told him my story from the time I crossed the river. The farm, the city, finding Bob. I didn't mention my experience of the dark world. "I'm just walking until I find my world, my purpose."

"And you'll find both," Conrad assured me. "We all do."

"And you, where is your world? What's your purpose?"

"I'm from the world of Iberis, and I'm a musician. Poppy, Lois, and I are on our way to Lobelia. I'm going to be playing at a rock concert there."

A rock concert. Really? They were going to a rock concert, in heaven, in a Volkswagen van from the sixties.

As my mind worked to absorb what I was hearing, I spotted the two girls and Bob making their way back toward us. Lois was carrying the bag, which now looked quite full, and Poppy had the water bottle, which appeared to be a lot heavier.

They sat down and the water was passed around. I had become familiar with this water. Cool, invigorating, and alive. Lois opened the bag and set it down between us. Apples, pears, purple plums, and loads of wild berries.

"Where did you find all this fruit?" I asked.

"It's everywhere," Poppy said. "You don't have to go far from the highway to find something to eat. And of course, there are rivers and streams everywhere with this amazing water."

As we sat and enjoyed the refreshments, my thoughts returned to the rock concert. I looked at the girls. "So, are you musicians, too, like Conrad? Are you going to be playing at the concert?"

"Oh no," Lois said. "We're just along for the ride, to keep Connie company and cheer him on when he's performing."

Connie? Hmm. I think I'll just keep calling him Conrad.

Poppy suddenly acted as if she'd had a brainwave. She was looking straight at me. "Hey, why don't you come with us? The concert is gonna be incredible. There'll be thousands of people there, and hundreds of musicians and singers."

I looked at Conrad and Lois. They both appeared as if they really wanted me to go with them.

"I don't know," I said. "What about Bob? I can't just leave him."

"No, of course not. Bob can come with us," Conrad said. "There's plenty of room in the van."

I took a bite of purple plum and leaned back with my hands behind me for support. I looked up and all around, wondering what I should do. Then something struck me as being rather amusing, and I was unable to

| Old Dogs, Children, and Watermelon Wine |

suppress a smile. I looked at the others and they seemed a little puzzled by my amusement.

Conrad spoke first. "So, Mickey, tell us what's so funny, man."

I didn't quite know what to say. I didn't want to offend anyone. "Look, this may not seem funny to you, but..."

"But what?" Poppy asked.

"Well, here I am, walking heaven's highway, and a bunch of hippies, in a Volkswagen van from the sixties, pull over and try to and talk me into going with them to a rock concert. If I went back to the world I came from and told people this story, they wouldn't believe me. They'd tell me I'd been dreaming."

The three of them looked at me for a few moments before having a little chuckle.

"I guess we've been here a long time," Lois said. "Thinking back to when I arrived, I remember expecting to be dressed in a white gown, floating around on a cloud, and ... that was it. I'm happy that heaven is way more fun than that."

Conrad leaned over and gave me a friendly punch on the shoulder. "A bunch of hippies, eh?"

The three of them looked at me expectantly, and I threw my hands in the air. "Okay, okay, I'm going with you. I'm going to a rock concert in heaven, with a bunch of hippies, in a Volkswagen van from the sixties. Who could refuse an offer like that?"

"That's settled then," Lois said, getting to her feet. Our thirst was quenched, and we'd had our fill of wild fruit. "It'll be the four of us, and Bob, of course. Let's get on the road."

We strolled back to the van. Lois got into the driver's seat, and Poppy sat beside her. Conrad and I seated ourselves on the bench seat behind them. Bob had lots of room in the back.

The Volkswagen started moving and we were on our way. The ride was smooth, and the van's motor was surprisingly quiet. I looked out the window and experienced a new perspective. The fields, the flowers, the trees, everything outside of the vehicle moved quickly past us, and it felt as if we were travelling at high speed. At the rate we were going, we would be in the next world in no time.

Conrad had taken his guitar from the roof rack and he began strumming. We all sang along, and I felt well pleased with having made the decision to join them.

Lois turned off the highway and the van took us in another direction. I leaned sideways and looked between Poppy and Lois at the road ahead. I saw little difference from the highway we'd just left. But now our destination was in sight. Directly ahead of us was a solid globe, a new world, and we were driving straight at it.

"There it is," Conrad said. "Lobelia, that's where we're headed, Mickey. That's where the concert is."

As this new world advanced upon us, my experience was as it had been when I approached Bellis. But travelling in the van, everything happened faster. Lobelia captured the full extent of my vision and eclipsed the universe

| Old Dogs, Children, and Watermelon Wine |

behind it. What had been a mighty sphere became flat land.

At first, the transition from heaven's highway into this new world seemed to go unnoticed. Then, without forewarning, there was a dramatic change in the outlook.

This world was brown, red, and gold, many different shades of only a few colours. A floor of sand was edged with mountains of rock, shaped beyond imagination. We were in a desert. It was a landscape that even a great artist could not duplicate.

I looked at my companions. Like me, they were silent, captivated by the desolate beauty. Brown, red, and gold, blended together beneath a ceiling of blue that held the stars, planets, solid globes, and translucent spheres blurred with colour.

As we moved quickly through this glorious landscape, it seemed the horizon off to our right was getting closer to us. But I was mistaken. It was not the horizon. As it became closer, I watched the desert give way to the ocean, an ocean as blue as the sky above, spread out flat and wide, meeting the sky in a barely distinguishable line. It was a landscape that begged for an audience.

Conrad broke the silence. With his gaze fixed on the magnificence, he said, "Now that's the work of the Master Artist."

I looked at him. "You mean God?"

"That's who I'm talking about, man; nobody else can do work like that."

Poppy turned to the driver. "Lois, stop the van. I'm going swimming."

Lois pulled over. "I'll join you," she said.

"Me too," said Conrad.

I looked around. I was desperate to get into the inviting water, but ... I looked at Conrad. "I don't have anything to wear for swimming."

"No worries, Mickey, I'll find something for you."

Conrad and I jumped out of the van, and he pulled two pairs of shorts out of a bag on the roof rack. He handed me a pair, and the two of us quickly got changed behind the van. We waited for the girls. They were soon out of the vehicle, swimsuits on, and ready for the water.

It was hot, but the heat was invigorating and in no way overpowering. Hot air carried by a sweet breeze. We walked across the warm sand, tasted the salt air, and embraced the soft wind coming off the ocean.

Bob didn't venture beyond the shallow water, but the rest of us were soon in up to our shoulders. The water was salty, buoyant, and just cool enough to be refreshing. We swam a little, none of us exerting ourselves too much. Mostly we just lay back in the water and allowed the gentle current to move us around.

I'm sure all of us would have been happy to stay longer, but Conrad seemed anxious to make a move. "We should get going," he said. "I need to be there before the concert starts."

Back on the road, Conrad had taken over the driving. I sat beside him, with Poppy and Lois sitting behind us. I felt renewed from the swim and was looking forward to the concert.

We turned off the highway and headed for a low range of hills in the distance. The ocean remained close, but as we approached the hills, the water disappeared behind the higher ground. Ahead, I saw a vast area shimmering like the ocean itself, light being reflected a thousand ways. A parking lot. A sea of vehicles, light reflecting off glass and polished surfaces.

"That's where we park," Conrad said.

I looked around as we drove toward the parking area. "I don't see anything but a parking lot," I said. "Where's the concert?"

Conrad pointed at the hillside. "We walk up there. When we get to the top, we'll be able to see it all. I tell you, Mickey, you've never been to a concert like this before."

He parked the Volkswagen, and we stepped down onto the desert sand, me in my canvas shoes. Lois, Poppy, and Conrad, with a guitar on each shoulder, remained barefoot. It was hot, but now without the relief of an ocean breeze.

We commenced the walk up. At the foot of the hillside, we stopped to admire a cluster of flowers. Small, delicate, and brightly coloured, thriving in the heat and with little moisture.

With Bob leading, we made our way between red rocks streaked with gold and miniature trees with orange leaves, healthy and vigorous in their natural environment.

There were people walking ahead of us, and others behind us. I remembered Poppy saying, "There'll be thousands of people there." There were certainly a lot of vehicles parked below, and I began to wonder just how many thousands of people would show up.

We were not far from the top when I felt it. The salty breeze, warm, yet it subdued the heat and refreshed the body. A few more steps and once again we would be in sight of the ocean.

CHAPTER 13

ROCK MY SOUL

From the top of the hill, I surveyed the arena. An amphitheatre, built into the hillside. It was shaped in a vast semicircle reaching from the ocean on one side and sweeping around to meet the ocean on the other side. Throughout the sloping hillside, the rock had naturally formed to create tiered benches that served the same purpose as would bleachers at a sports field.

At the bottom of the hill was an elevated area. It looked like a small mountain that had been cut off flat, leaving it a little higher than the ground around it. Its surface was smooth, shiny, and reflective, like black glass. It was the stage from which the musicians would be playing, big enough to hold hundreds of people. It was this natural platform that held back the ocean behind it, an ocean that flooded out to the horizon in all directions.

Dozens of people were on the stage tinkering with equipment, tuning instruments, and generally preparing for the concert. The size of the arena was overwhelming, yet as I looked around, there didn't appear to be a bad seat in the house. Each position had an unobstructed view of the stage.

Tens of thousands of people had already gathered, and more were making their way down the hill. All over the amphitheatre, small tent-like structures had been erected, from which food and drinks were being served.

"So, Mickey, what do you think?" Conrad asked. "Pretty cool venue for a concert, eh."

"You've got that right," I replied. "I never expected anything like this. Tell me, how long will the concert last?"

"Well, we've got loads of performers. We'll be playing all night for sure."

Night, something I'd not experienced since crossing the river. I'd slept, but had not experienced the end of a day, or a morning, or what lay between the two.

Conrad interrupted my thoughts. Looking toward the stage, he said, "I'd better head down there, I need to get together with my band and prepare for our performance."

Lois grabbed one of Conrad's guitars. "I'll go with you," she said.

| Old Dogs, Children, and Watermelon Wine |

As the two of them made their way down to the stage, Poppy called after them. "Play well, Connie!"

We watched them navigate their way down the slope. When they reached the bottom, I turned to Poppy and asked, "Poppy, how long exactly is all night? How long does a night last?"

She seemed to be thinking hard about this, but eventually replied, "I'm not sure, not exactly. At least until morning." She was looking at me and appeared serious, but was then unable to suppress a giggle.

"Until morning," I repeated. "Very funny, I'm sure."

That was it. I'm not asking any more questions about time or distance. I was convinced that in this world, they did not exist.

Poppy spotted some people she knew and asked me to go with her to meet them.

"You go ahead," I said. "I'm going to take a walk around the arena. I'll catch up with you later."

She made a beeline for her friends, and I looked around for Bob. He was close by and making his way toward me. He was chewing on something and looked pleased with himself. Someone had been feeding him again. There was no danger of this dog ever going hungry.

We had entered the stadium on the right side. Bob and I set off, walking toward the other side. The stage was the centrepiece, fixed on the very edge of the ocean, restraining the body of water behind it. With the hillside wrapped around the stage, the perfect amphitheatre had been created. Given its size, it would take us a while to reach the other side.

People on the other side of the arena seemed far away, but those on the stage were easily identifiable. I could see Conrad chatting with a small group, who I assumed to be the members of his band.

I stopped at one of the little booths and got a tall fruit drink. The man who served me seemed happy in his work. "Plenty more where that came from," he said. Then laughing at his own humour, added, "Refills are free."

I laughed with him, but was still not entirely comfortable with accepting everything offered to me without having to pay for it. I walked on a little farther before taking a seat in the "bleachers" to enjoy my juice.

A small group of people stopped beside me. "This seems like a good spot," one of them said. Looking at me, he asked, "Mind if we sit with you?"

By the time he had finished speaking, they were all seated anyway. I didn't mind at all. They paid attention to Bob, and I got a couple of slaps on the back accompanied by, "Good to see you," and "This is gonna be fun."

I looked at the sea of people around me, more people in one place than I'd ever seen before. As my eyes wandered around the stadium, I became aware of the fading light. Evening was approaching. The arena and all those in it had become less visible, but the stage was flooded with light. Above me, it seemed as if the stars, the suns of the universe, had turned their light away from the world around us and focused it on the stage below. Its dark mirrored surface reflected everything upon it. The musicians and their instruments were now accompanied by their perfectly duplicated shadows on the polished rock.

The ocean beyond had darkened but now boldly reflected the universe that watched over it. The stars, motionless above, now jostled for position on the surface of the water. The twilight lingered, and it became evident that this was as dark as it was going to get.

I turned my attention to the stage. It was ablaze as if illuminated by a hundred giant spotlights. The musicians, the singers, all the performers easily identifiable by an audience of thousands. The number of people on the stage was down to about fifteen. This was the opening band, and they looked about ready to start playing. Seven musicians, a lead singer, and half a dozen backing singers.

The first notes were heard, and the band launched into their opening number. The audience was immediately caught up in the music. Classic rock, a hard rhythmic beat without anger or aggression, performed by gifted entertainers. They completed their opening number to thunderous applause, then moved straight into the next song.

I watched the drummer, the keyboard player, all the musicians and singers, and was mesmerized by the light from above casting their shadows in multiple directions across the stage. Each shadow mimicked their every move in a natural display of special effects.

As the band played, the intensity of the music gained momentum, and the audience was right with them. When they closed out their set with a rock 'n'roll classic, everyone was on their feet clapping, cheering, and whistling. It had been quite a performance, and it took a while before the audience allowed the band to leave the stage.

During a short break in the music, I listened to the buzz of conversation around me. People were making their way toward the little food tents. Others remained seated, waiting for the music to resume. Above, the stars rested silently in a shaded sky, as if watching over us.

Below, a new group of entertainers were making their way up to the stage, and I saw that Conrad was among them. They assumed their positions, and the applause died in anticipation. Conrad stepped to centre stage and opened with a solo instrumental performance. The crowd remained silent throughout, captivated by the artistry of a brilliant musician. When he closed out his piece, the people went wild. The ovation was long, and it was some time before the band could get into their next song.

When Conrad's band completed their final number, he stepped forward and made an announcement. "Okay, folks, it's time to make some noise for the Master."

People from all over the amphitheatre began making their way toward the stage, many of them carrying musical instruments. Saxophones, guitars, clarinets, and more. They made their way up to the stage, and spread out across the glassy surface. Each of them took up a position on

| Old Dogs, Children, and Watermelon Wine |

the platform as if they had rehearsed. Or perhaps it was something they had done many times before. When they were all in position there were at least three hundred of them. I wondered how they could possibly all play and sing together in time and in rhythm.

But they could, beautifully. Hundreds of voices from the stage joined by thousands more from around the stadium praising the Almighty, the Creator of the universe, the Master. Everyone was on their feet, waving their hands in the air, and some were dancing. Song after song was sung, songs of praise and worship, and everyone was part of it. Then from the stage, I heard words that were so familiar to me, words that I had sung many times, words that could never be lost, could never be left behind.

O Lord my God, when I in awesome wonder,
Consider all the worlds thy hands have made,
I see the stars, I hear the rolling thunder,
Thy power throughout the universe displayed.

I looked up and there they were. The stars, the planets, the worlds, formed and fixed in place by the Creator's hands.

How great thou art was repeated for the last time and, as if prompted by the words of the hymn, there was a flash of lightning followed immediately by a clap of thunder. The light lingered, illuminating the world around us. Then it was gone.

As if blinded by the light, the people were silent, but not for long. Suddenly, they broke into a deafening chorus of cheering, shouting, yelling, and whistling. Not wanting to be left out, I joined in.

When the noise died down enough to be heard, I turned to the woman beside me. "What was that?" I asked. "The thunder, the flash of lightening? Where did that come from?"

The lady looked up. "That was the Master," she said. "He's out there in another world, but he's watching us. He's always watching us. He was just saying . . . Thanks for the music."

I too looked up. So, he was out there in another world, and he just said, "Thanks for the music." Would I ever get to meet this Master of the universe? How would I find him? Would he find me?

The musicians and singers began leaving the stage, and before long only a few remained. They were the next performers on the schedule.

The music played on, one band after another. Small groups, large groups, and solo artists. All of them performing to an energized audience of a hundred thousand.

I'd been sitting and enjoying the music for who knows how long when I decided it was time to take a walk and try to find Conrad and the girls. Bob and I got to our feet and headed back in the direction from which we'd come. I stopped at a little booth, picked up a snack, and moved slowly on, scanning the area in the hope of finding my

| Old Dogs, Children, and Watermelon Wine |

friends. I was beginning to think that it was not going to be easy finding them among all these people. Then I spotted all three of them sitting together watching the stage.

Before I reached them, Poppy saw me and waved me over. "We were beginning to wonder where you were," she said. "What do you think of the concert?"

"Never seen anything like it before," I replied. "What a show." I gave Conrad a slap on the back. "Great playing, man."

Oh no! I was talking like him now.

As we enthused over the concert, the sky began to lighten and the stars were disappearing from the water. Night was coming to an end. A new day was about to begin.

Conrad looked around. "The concert will be ending soon. Do you want to travel on with me, Mickey?"

"Where are you going?" I asked.

"Statice. I'm playing in a hockey tournament there. I'm the goalie."

Statice. The world where it's always winter, the perfect world for skiing and skating and the like. I looked at Lois and Poppy. "What are you girls doing?"

"I'm gonna hang out here with friends for a while," Poppy said. "Lois is going with Connie."

"I'm not a big hockey fan," Lois added. "But I hope to do a little skiing."

I was torn as to what to do, but I made the decision. "You know, I'd love to join you, Conrad, but I think

I'll just keep walking. I need to find my world, and I don't think Statice is it. I'm hoping to find somewhere a little warmer."

We said our goodbyes. As usual, Bob got most of the attention. Poppy even became a little tearful.

At the top of the arena, before we headed down the hill, I turned around. They were watching us leave.

Just a bunch of hippies, driving from one world to another, in a Volkswagen van from the sixties, man.

CHAPTER 14

DESERT STORM

Bob and I made our way down the slope, leaving the concert in the desert behind us. We reached the paved road and soon fell into our usual routine. Me walking on the pavement, Bob on the sandy shoulder. It had become fully light, a new day, clear and bright. The sky was bluer than ever, with the occasional cloud, woolly, white, and nonthreatening. Before long, we were back on the main highway, the highway that would take us from Lobelia into the next world.

As we walked, the heat of the desert intensified, and I wondered how long it would be before we found water and shade. It was hot, but not overpowering or unbearable. The heat seemed to carry an energy with it, and I felt empowered by its strength.

Trees were nonexistent in this landscape, but clusters of small shrubs and flowers appeared to be remarkably healthy. In the dry desert earth, it seemed they were able to find all that was required for them to survive.

Then I felt it. The warm breeze and the taste of salt on my lips. I turned my head, and once again the ocean was in view, a shining sea, a dazzling jewel in the desert. I stopped, turned toward the ocean, and embraced the wind, which carried relief off the cool water.

Again, the road saw little traffic. A few cars stopped. People asked if I was okay. Did I need a ride? One man stopped and gave me a wide-brimmed hat. "You need one of these in this heat." He'd said.

With my hat on, we continued our journey. My eyes strained to see ahead, searching for any evidence of the desert coming to an end. There was no end in sight but, in the distance I did see something. It was something that didn't seem to fit with the desert land around it. Something that looked out of place, that had been put there with little thought given to how it might blend in with all that surrounded it.

As we drew closer, it became apparent that we were approaching an area of prolific growth. A small forest, it would seem. Trees, their branches heavy with foliage, lush and green. Beneath the trees, no grass grew, but flowers of many colours were plentiful.

| Old Dogs, Children, and Watermelon Wine |

We walked into this oasis and soon discovered the reason for the abundant growth. Water flowed from beneath a wide flat rock, filling a shallow pool. From the pool, the water seeped out to the red soil, thereby creating the fertile growth around us.

We quenched our thirst at the pool, and Bob settled himself in the shade of a leafy tree. I ventured a little deeper into the oasis. It was humid and fragrant, quiet but for the high-pitched chatter of a pair of birds, unseen, among the branches.

I peered through an opening in the trees at the desert beyond. The abrupt contrast in the landscape was startling. While seemingly unfitting, it was as if this little haven of shade, with its cool water flowing from the desert floor, was here by design. A place of relief and rest for those who traveled the desert highway. I walked slowly around and was soon back to where I'd started.

Bob looked as if he'd had a nap, seeming alert and ready to move on. "Come on, Bob, let's go." He lifted his head and looked up and all around, first one way then the other. After this "checking out" of the surroundings, he lowered his head onto his paws. Clearly, he was not interested in going anywhere. I knew when his mind was made up, there was little I could do to change it. "Okay, Bob, I'm leaving. I'll walk slow. You catch up to me when you're ready."

I stepped out onto the highway and resumed the walk across the desert. I'd covered only a short distance when

I felt something land on my head. I raised my hand but felt nothing. I looked up and, one after another, they landed on my face. Raindrops, big and heavy, and the down-pouring was gaining momentum. In moments, the rain had become torrential. I turned and ran as fast as I could back to the oasis, taking shelter under the tree where Bob still lay.

He looked up at me, and his expression told me he knew it was going to rain, he knew I was going to get wet. That's why he had refused to walk with me. I looked down at him, and I was pretty sure he was laughing at me.

My clothes were soaked through. It felt wonderful. In this atmosphere, I knew they would dry in no time.

I sat down beside Bob and leaned back against the trunk of the tree. The rain poured down, but the tree protected us. The water ran from one leaf to another and drained off in a circle around us. It was as if we were sitting under a giant umbrella.

Beyond our shelter the sight was magnificent. The rain pounding on the desert floor created a mist that stayed low to the ground, and the sky above remained visible and blue. A scent lifted off the wet desert sand, a perfume that suggested this was the first rain in a long time. A desert storm.

I rested my head against the tree and listened to the rain. As I listened, my thoughts took me back over a journey that had brought me this far. The '57 Chevy and watermelon wine. A dinner party for fifty people. A

| Old Dogs, Children, and Watermelon Wine |

thousand children, a little beekeeper and finding Bob. Then came the hippies in the multi-coloured Volkswagen van, and the rock concert in the desert.

The intensity of the storm weakened, and before long the rain had stopped. It became silent, and I had a sense that the atmosphere had taken on a new energy. It was as if the very air that I was breathing had been recharged.

Out across the desert, the low mist had been replaced by a steamy fog that rose up, then dissolved in midair. I felt renewed and was confident that I could walk far without fear of fatigue.

Although motivated, and without reason not to move on, Bob and I remained where we were.

CHAPTER 15

BURNT OUT

Without knowing how long I'd been sitting there, I became aware that it had become cold and quite dark, as if in the latter stages of twilight. I eased myself to my feet, my body stiff from lack of movement. I stretched in an effort to loosen my limbs and, through the semi-darkness, surveyed my surroundings.

I looked into the little oasis, but the light was such that I saw the trees only as black outlines against a darkening sky. In the other direction, the golden sand of the desert was now a blackened platform, empty and wide.

| Old Dogs, Children, and Watermelon Wine |

I took a few steps into the oasis and was sickened by the stench of damp charcoal. It was then that I saw the trees were not darkened by the fading light. A fire had gone through and consumed the foliage leaving only bare trunks and branches.

I walked out of the trees and into the desert, but this was not the desert. It was the field where the elk once grazed. Its pasture was burnt and black and showed no signs of new growth.

Behind me were not the trees of the little oasis, but the tall firs standing at the foot of the hills that lay beyond. Ahead of me, what was once grassland was no more.

The landscape, once so familiar to me, was now beyond recognition. But I knew. There was no doubt.

I was back.

I looked out across the burnt earth in the direction of my house, but the darkness was such that it remained out of sight.

I started walking, anxious to return to the warmth of the home I loved. As my legs began to hurt, I could see through the darkness the gateway that allowed access to the gravel road. But the gate was gone. Only two charred posts remained. I reached the opening and leaned against a blackened post in an effort to relieve my legs of the weight they carried. The distances I was able to walk were getting shorter, and I was eager to get inside the house.

I looked across the gravel road but saw only a mass of dark forest outlined against a dark sky. My house should have been right there, in front of the trees, but all I could see was a dark space. A sickening panic hit me hard, and I looked around, wondering if I'd made a mistake. Perhaps in the darkness I'd lost my way. But I knew that was not possible. I was home, but my home was not there. It was gone.

I walked hesitantly across the road and on to what was my driveway. It was uneven, wet, and muddy. I carefully made my way up the incline and stood where my house once stood.

While darkness continued to fall, I was able to see that, all around me, unlike the field and the woods below, there had been new growth since the fire. Coarse bramble had sprouted from the burned earth, their thorny vines spread out across the ground as if trying to cover up, to hide, what once existed there.

I moved a few steps to one side and sat on a charred log, a fir brought down by the fire. It was about where I would sit in my living room and look out at a green field and the wildlife that grazed there, and at the woods beyond the field and the gently sloping hillside behind the trees. Everything I once loved was in ruins, destroyed, gone. I placed my head in my hands and remained where I was, motionless.

My wretched despair was interrupted by distant voices, dull monotone sounds that were coming from up the road. I waited, still and silent, watching for the darkness to reveal someone or something. I watched the road, my eyes straining and unblinking. I could no longer hear voices and was beginning to think that whoever they were, they'd turned around and were now heading away from me.

Then, through the darkness I glimpsed movement on the road. Moments later, I was able to make out the dark outlines of three people. They walked silently now. All three were wearing dark clothes, jackets with hoods that covered their heads and faces.

As they were about to pass my driveway, I called out to them. "Could you help me?" They did not stop, nor did the hooded heads turn in my direction. It was as if I had not spoken, or they had not heard me. They just continued in the direction they were going.

I stood up and jogged down the drive to the road. Again, I called out to them. "Who are you? Where are you going?" Still they continued on. Still, they made no attempt to respond.

I soon caught up to them and, puzzled as to why they were ignoring me, I reached out and took one of them by the arm. In an instant a woman's face turned toward me. I was shocked by what I saw. Her skin was a ghostly white. Her eyes were black and, although seemingly lifeless, they reflected unreserved fear, a fear unlike any I'd witnessed before.

She pulled her arm away, raised it up across her face, and shrank away from me. It was as if she thought I was about to strike her. The two who were with her never once looked in my direction, and the one I'd reached out to turned away from me. Without speaking a word, the three of them walked on, disappearing into the darkness.

I returned to my seat and waited for the nightmare to end. But it wasn't going to end. It was real.

Again, I heard the sound of approaching voices, and again I navigated my way down to the roadside. Perhaps this time someone would stop and talk to me and tell me what had happened to my world.

I caught a glimpse of the pale faces first, then the hooded outlines of four people. As they drew closer, their methodical pace slowed even more before they came to a stop a few steps from where I was standing.

Three of them made an effort to hide their faces, but the fourth seemed a little more self-assured and looked directly at me.

I pointed at the spot where my house once stood. "I used to live there but my house is gone. What happened to it?"

To my relief, the man spoke. "When the fire came through, it took everything."

"And you? What about you?" I asked. "Your skin is so pale and your eyes are black, like coal. What's wrong? What happened to you?" I made as if to move a little closer, but right away he raised both hands, palms facing toward me.

"Stop. Keep away from us."

I advanced no farther, taken aback by his demands. "I don't understand. What are you afraid of?"

| Old Dogs, Children, and Watermelon Wine |

He turned momentarily to the dark figures beside him, then looked back at me. "We have the sickness. Stay away from us."

I looked at him, the blanched pallor, the black eyes; there was no doubt. Like the woman I'd encountered before, an illness was upon him. "How many of you have the sickness?" I asked.

"We all have it. No one was spared. It was carried by the smoke from the fire, and it fell on everyone. But you don't have it. You don't have the sickness. You should go back to where you came from. Go now, before you become like us."

I pressed him further. "This sickness, is there no cure?"

"We were told there was a cure, but we were afraid. Everyone was afraid. We thought it would harm us, so we refused it; we wouldn't accept the cure. Now it's too late."

He turned away, and the four of them resumed walking, their steps slow and weary. I called after them. "Where are you going?"

The one I'd been speaking with stopped and turned around, a dark figure, and again I was sickened by the ghastly pallor.

"We're going to look at the light." He paused for a moment before adding, "Go back to where you came from . . . while you still can."

I watched as they vanished into the darkness, four wretched people in a burnt-out world. Was I now one of them? I returned to the fallen log and sat. My only thoughts were of leaving this place. I stared at my feet wondering how.

"What are you doing here?"

My head jerked up, and I focused my eyes on the road. In moments, through the darkness, the outline of a person materialized. He was tall, wearing light-coloured clothing. A thin man, wearing a hat with a brim. His skin was not pale like the others. He was not looking directly at me, but his head was erect and his profile dark.

He spoke again. "You don't belong here. Go back to where you came from."

Go back to where you came from. That was the second time I'd heard those words on this horrible night. I looked up and all around, my mind searching. Then it came to me. A recall of another place, another time.

"Marcus!" As I shouted his name, I looked back to the gravel road, but there was no one there. I looked one way, then the other, but was unable to see anyone. I called his name again, but there was no response. The tall thin man may have been my only hope, but he was gone.

I repeated those words to myself. "Go back to where you came from." Where did I come from? How do I get back there?

I tried to see out across the field, but the night was unyielding. It was as if a wall of darkness was rising up and eclipsing all that was once visible. The trees and the mountain beyond appeared as a single black mass painted on a charcoal canvas. A hair-thin line of light, as if drawn with a fine pencil, separated the black hilltop from a charcoal sky. The razor line of light illuminated nothing. But could it possibly be a promise of what lay beyond?

I stood and made my way down the muddy driveway, across the road, and between the burned gate posts. Unable to see where I was going, I kept my eyes on the thin line of light. I stumbled forward, my eyes irritating from the ash drifting up from the burnt earth.

Then I felt it, the feeling I'd come to dread. The pain in my legs had returned. As I walked, it seemed to worsen with each step. My pace slowed, and I was barely able to place one foot in front of the other. I laboured to push myself forward, but to no avail. My legs ceased to function. It was as if each foot had dropped an anchor, anchors that had buried themselves deep into the blackened ground.

I stood there, held hostage in a dying world, without hope of release. Despairingly, I lifted my head and saw again the line of light that traced the mountain top. It had weakened, faded, and was almost gone. It seemed likely that, before long it would disappear completely.

"God help me!" I shouted out the words, wondering if the Almighty could hear me. Probably not. Even so, I called out again. "God help me!"

I closed my eyes and tried to shut out the pain.

Miraculously, it worked. The pain subsided and I felt as if I could walk. But it was not to be. Both feet were still anchored firmly to the ground. My eyes remained closed, and my despair deepened.

After standing motionless for an indeterminable period of time, I felt something around my ankles. It was like a stiff breeze close to the ground. I looked down and could just about see my blackened canvas shoes. The ground on which I stood seemed to be alive. My eyes focused, and I realized that the earth was moving below me. The black dirt in front of me, as far as I could see, was moving toward me. Then, like the belt on a treadmill, it passed beneath my feet.

Yet I remained where I was. I tried to see what was ahead of me. While I had not moved, the black mass that was the woodland and the hill beyond was close and speeding toward me. The thin line of light was sharper and clearer, but still it shed no light on the darkness around me.

Dark silhouettes of the tree-line rushed toward me. As they approached, I held my arms across my face for protection. The ugly black shapes flew past, burnt branches brushed roughly against me. I was on a nightmare ride through a forest on an express train.

Soon the woods were behind me, yet the darkness continued to advance. It seemed to be on a mission to destroy me.

But perhaps not.

Looking up, I saw that the horizon of light was wide, bright, and alive. And it was coming for me.

Like a mighty soundless explosion, it hit me. Again I raised my forearms across my face, this time to shield my eyes from the brilliant light of a thousand new worlds.

CHAPTER 16

STRANGER EN ROUTE

With a measure of trepidation, I opened my eyes, expecting the light and all its brilliance to flood my vision. But I remained in darkness. I felt a surge of anxiety; had my escape been no more than a deceitful fabrication, a manipulation of my tattered emotions?

As I regained my senses, I realized that my forearms were pressed firmly across my face, shutting out my field of vision. Cautiously, I lowered them. It was then that the light streamed in.

I rose to my feet and looked around, searching for any evidence of the dark and dying world that was once my home.

As my mind cleared, my being calmed in the assurance that it was a world I'd left long ago. A world to which I would never return. A dark realm from which I would forever be protected.

Defying explanation, I had been given a window on that world one last time, and it was shown to be powerless to hold me. That was not my place. My place was here.

I looked into the little oasis, its rich and abundant growth supported by the relentless flow of water from the desert floor. Across the desert, the barren desolation was uncompromised by greenery or evidence of human existence. Following the rain, the heat had returned, and remnants of the steamy fog became lost in the atmosphere.

Above and all around, a clear sky was decorated with stars, planets, globes. Some appearing solid and having substance, others a source of light and warmth. There were spheres that were translucent and blurred with colour, appearing as soap bubbles blown through a ring.

It was a magical universe, and it was where I belonged. My world was here.

I looked around for Bob, but he was nowhere in sight. "Bob!" I called his name, but still, he didn't appear. I made my way to the little pool, thinking he may have gone for a drink, but there was no sign of him. I wasn't worried; I

| Old Dogs, Children, and Watermelon Wine |

knew he would show up sooner or later. He was probably lying in the shade somewhere, sleeping.

I quenched my thirst and returned to the tree beside the highway. I sat and waited for Bob to show up.

My eyes searched the highway, a grey stripe that seemed to go on forever. It was empty; there was no traffic. No one travelling on foot like me.

Then something caught my eye. Far away, I detected movement in the desert, beside the highway. My eyes searched the barren expanse, and in moments focused on what appeared to be a white cloud, flat and close to the ground. It was some distance from the road, and although it remained still, I kept my eyes on it.

Then the cloud moved, slowly at first. Then, with a sudden burst of speed, it raced diagonally across the desert, almost reaching the highway before sweeping away from the road and again coming to rest some distance from the pavement. Now that it was closer, I could see that it was not a cloud but a team of white horses, about a hundred of them. A hundred horses, white and wild, moving together as one. It was a magnificent sight.

I watched them, waiting for their next move, hoping they would continue to advance in my direction. I was eager to see this spectacle at close quarters.

As I waited, I looked back up the highway. Again something caught my attention, this time on the other side of the road. Although high above and in the distance, I could determine what it was. Birds of prey, eagles, their numbers equaling that of the wild horses. They moved slowly through the atmosphere. Little by little, they were getting closer to me, turning vast circles in the sky. Their outstretched wings were wide and showed no sign of movement.

On one side, the horses, for the moment, remained still. On the other side, the eagles circled.

My eyes were drawn back to the highway and, at the same distance away, I saw a lone figure walking in my direction. Someone walking alone, flanked on one side by birds of prey, on the other side by a team of white horses. It was an impressive entourage.

While still in the distance, it became clear that it was the walk of a man. As he advanced, my curiosity deepened. The eagles and the horses would move ahead of him, then linger a while until he caught up before moving forward once again. Throughout, they kept their distance from the solitary traveler.

As he drew closer, I observed that he was a man of little more than average height, and he walked with his head held high. His stride was long and unhurried, and he maintained an even pace. As he walked, his head turned one way then the other, surveying the surroundings; reminiscent of a landlord taking inventory of his estate.

His demeanor was that of confidence, and he had about him a proprietary air. Even from some distance away, it was evident that this was a man who knew where he was, where he was going, and how to get there.

| Old Dogs, Children, and Watermelon Wine |

As the eagles and horses remained vigilant, I saw two birds the size of doves circling above the stranger's head. They too, like the entourage, would fly ahead, then wait. I watched, fascinated by the attention this man was getting.

Abruptly, he stopped and looked up at the two birds above his head. He watched them for a moment, then reached into a pocket, withdrew his hand, and stretched it out, palm open. The birds circled once more before one of them swooped down and took something from his outstretched hand. The second one quickly followed suit.

The entourage advanced, but not before the walking had resumed. The horses reached my position and waited quietly in the desert across the road. The eagles circled directly above me.

I could see now that the walker had long windswept hair that reached almost to his shoulders, and his beard was cut close. His clothing was the colour of the desert sand. His shirt was untucked, with buttons down the front, the top two and the bottom two undone. His sleeves were rolled up to the elbow. Loose fitting like his shirt, his trousers hung to just above his sandals, revealing ankles as suntanned as his face and forearms.

Then he stopped and fixed his gaze on me. The entourage was silent, and the two doves settled in the tree above me. Standing where he was, he was still too far away for me to see his eyes or any distinguishable features. But his presence demanded attention.

I felt the need to get to my feet and began to ease myself off the ground. I was half-way up when, inexplicably, my legs gave way and I dropped to my knees. I knew that this was not the return of the affliction I once had, but I remained as I was anyway: on my knees, staring at the ground, and feeling a little foolish.

As I knelt there, I heard footsteps coming toward me. When they stopped, I sensed he was close. I kept my head down and waited. A few moments of silence passed. Then the stranger spoke.

"Michael, I thought you had a dog. Where is he?"

Did this man know me? Perhaps he was not a stranger. He knew my name, and he knew I had a dog. Maybe I did know him.

Slowly, I lifted my head. Then just as slowly, I raised my eyes.

Oh ... My ... God.

EPILOGUE

TODAY

I watch him as he walks away, the confident stride, the upright posture. On the ground, the team of white horses match his pace. In the air, the birds of prey circle, keeping vigil. The doves stay close.

I watch him go.

The Master... Lord of the universe... God on foot.

A stranger no more.

As the horses blend into a cloud and the eagles become as sparrows, he vanishes into a mirage of shimmering glass.

I make my way back to the spring and sit on the gently sloping bank beside the pool. I sit upright, my knees against my chest, and look through the clear water. The pool has a sandy bottom, and the water magnifies a multitude of tiny reflective particles and coloured pebbles.

I have my instructions now. I know what is required of me. I've been given a purpose. I know the role that I'm to play.

The ones I love are all here now. I'm to go and find my world and seek them out.

Then I feel him beside me, his tail slapping against my thigh. "Bob."

He looks at me, appearing somewhat apologetic for having wandered off. However, any guilt he may have is short lived. He makes himself comfortable, lowers his head onto his paws, and closes his eyes.

I lean back, and my head settles in the fragrant undergrowth. As if knowing that I need to rest, the sky dims, and a peaceful twilight descends upon me.

I gaze into the universe and become lost in wonder of all that surrounds me. As my eyelids become heavy, the stars dissolve, blend together, and become as one. I try to keep them in focus, but little by little they melt away into a purple sky.

My sleep is sweet; my dreams of old dogs, children, and watermelon wine.

AUTHOR'S NOTE

I refuse to allow my meagre understanding, and modest imagination, to place limitations upon what heaven may or may not be.

ACKNOWLEDGEMENTS

For casting a critical eye, my thanks to:
DOROTHY ISTED, CHARLENE MADDEN,
and EUGENE PIRIE.

CREDITS

Old Dogs, Children, and Watermelon Wine.
    Song written by: TOM T. HALL.

How Great Thou Art.
    Hymn written by: CARL BOBERG.
    Translated by: STUART K. HINE.
    Sung by millions.

ABOUT THE AUTHOR

Photo: Sherri Spiers.

JAMES MICHAEL SPIERS, (Jim) is originally from England, and has been married to Pam since 1974. They have one son, two daughters, and three grandchildren. Formerly a farmer and an innkeeper, he is retired and lives in British Columbia, Canada.

Mailto: piccadillyjim53@gmail.com

Printed in Canada